# GEOFF PAGE

# BENTON'S CONVICTION

# ABOUT *UNTAPPED*

Most Australian books ever written have fallen out of print and become unavailable for purchase or loan from libraries. This includes important local and national histories, biographies and memoirs, beloved children's titles, and even winners of glittering literary prizes such as the Miles Franklin Literary Award.

Supported by funding from state and territory libraries, philanthropists and the Australian Research Council, *Untapped* is identifying Australia's culturally important lost books, digitising them, and promoting them to new generations of readers. As well as providing access to lost books and a new source of revenue for their writers, the *Untapped* collaboration is supporting new research into the economic value of authors' reversion rights and book promotion by libraries, and the relationship between library lending and digital book sales. The results will feed into public policy discussions about how we can better support Australian authors, readers and culture.

See untapped.org.au for more information, including a full list of project partners and rediscovered books.

*Readers are reminded that these books are products of their time. Some may contain language or reflect views that might now be found offensive or inappropriate.*

For my family and in memory of Rev. B. Linden Webb

# ACKNOWLEDGEMENTS

Acknowledgement is made to: Rodney Wetherell, Ann-Mari Jordens, Michael McKernan and members of the library and publications staff of the Australian War Memorial for invaluable help with research; Alan Gould for critical comments on the manuscript; the University of Wollongong for a visiting lectureship during which a portion of this novel was written; and the Literature Board of the Australia Council for a general writing grant on which the novel was completed.

### Author's note

While this novel refers to and is based on a number of real events all the characters, including those holding particular offices, are fictional.

# PART ONE

PART ONE

## I

Benton, at the very top now, collected his breath and looked north. The mist had risen, vanished, though it was still palpable in the air. The morning was almost windless, the smoke from Geradgery's few hundred kitchens tilted slightly to the east. The paddocks, browning with the May frosts, flowed out either way from the town's close grid and rolled by stages towards forested skylines. A pair of forceps, Benton had often thought, looking down at the twin strips of road and rail which passed as handles on either side of Bald Knob, hinged at the town below him, then ran together northwards to disappear finally through a niche in the trees towards Glen Innes. Southwards the road became a cutting, winding down among scrappy trees towards Armidale. The railway, at a patient angle, climbed the valley's other side, a triumph of geometry in the chaos of minor gullies. Difficult to imagine Geradgery without them. How else might it be knotted to the world? From here on Bald Knob, the town's content with itself was almost visible, a kind of ramshackle perfection. He savoured again that residue of colour in the park and by the church. A morning like this in late autumn (Benton might once have said) could be God's manifesto to the world.

The roughness of the granite meanwhile came cold through the seat of his pants. He wondered how visible he'd be up here, how recognisable—a black crow maybe (with a white collar?). That last abandoned scramble up lichen and granite was, he knew, a little less than seemly but who was there to care up here? A parson might be forgiven an oddity or two, a fine tradition after all. Long walks were known to clear the mind; a sharp climb even more so.

Looking now, with such a mind, at the foot of the cutting,

he saw a windscreen's flash. And there on his rock, lost to all commitment, Benton watched the car's slow climb, its reappearance and disappearance on turn after turn, until at length it chugged self-consciously below him, a long, well-polished, boat-like sedan with what from here seemed a small blue flag fluttering on its bow.

Two hours later in his drawing room Benton glanced again at its passenger, this polished, taut man perched on the edge of the sofa. The pink cheeks were shaved to a mirror finish; the thin moustache had a similar edge. *Naturally*, said the accompanying letter, *I expect you will give our friend and associate, Captain Winters, every assistance and trust to hear no more of that little embarrassment we discussed last week.*

The captain was back on his feet again, pacing.

'Fine man, the bishop,' he asserted in a parade-ground staccato. 'Same school, you know. He was in the Upper Sixth when I was in Remove.' He looked impatiently out the window but appeared to see nothing. 'Good footballer, too. Nothing namby-pamby about him.' He stared again, briefly, at Benton as though the same might not apply there.

Benton, ignoring the stare, said nothing, distracted even more by the memory of that moment a week ago when the footballer in question had so amiably swept him into his well-leathered study and sat him down by the episcopal desk for some straight-shouldered advice.

'The sergeant and I ...' said Winters, suddenly more hesitant. 'We're rather depending on you, you know. We like the clergy to be involved. Can make quite a difference, especially to the ... waverers.' He paused, as if to give Benton time to make up his mind. 'The School of Arts is all lined up, no problem there.' Benton, respectful enough but still resistant, looked past him into the hall and in the quick silence heard the scrape of an iron pot coming off the stove. 'Councillor McLennan has already agreed to join us. And we'll be showing the new picture film,

*Heroes of the Dardanelles.*' The captain seemed to think that ought to clinch it but, seeing it hadn't, alighted once more on the sofa and, looking at Benton as if he alone might somehow be responsible, continued: 'I understand there are still quite a few eligibles in the district. McLennan reckons on fifty or sixty, in Geradgery alone.'

'Could be,' said Benton slowly, fielding Winters' irritation. 'Most people have someone who's gone—and a few lost at Gallipoli, if it comes to that.'

'Good turnout for the commemoration though,' Winters suggested abruptly. 'The bishop thought it was all rather splendid ... for a town of just a few hundred.' As the man sat there lightly banging the end of his swagger stick into his palm, Benton almost languidly looked past him through the tight squares of the window to where the sergeant was checking something under one of the raised bonnets of the car. Even under the pressure of Winters' impatience, something of that recent dawn commemoration came filtering back: the cold, rising light, the ricochet of his own voice, the small half-circle of bent women down the front. When Winters cut back in Benton had trouble remembering what he'd been talking about.

'... says you played quite a role last year in the rush after the Landing. Nothing like a stiff sermon to get them going, eh?' Benton was aware that the same condescension would not have been tried on the bishop.

Suddenly Winters seemed not only nervous but uncomfortable. A two-year-old boy stood in the hall doorway, attended somehow by a whiff of pea soup. A gentlemen, it seemed, could stay no longer. Snapping to his feet, as if a hint were an order, Winters concluded: 'No problem about Saturday then. Be in touch on the day. Five minutes should be enough.'

Benton stood up lankily to let his guest out, but the captain was already out the door, down the steps and short-cutting across the lawn as the sergeant stooped over the crank handle. Seconds later, as Benton and his son stood in the doorway, the car with its little blue flag whirled away down the road, the captain bestowing a clipped half salute in farewell. Gathering up his son, Benton turned and walked back down the hall to the kitchen. His wife was cutting bread near the sink—thick white chunks. He put the boy down, swung in and embraced her from behind, hands on her belly, pulling the fullness of her worsted beam up hard against his upper legs. Nuzzling in her dark brown hair, he could feel the invisible smile on her face. 'Me too, me too!' cried Billyjim, cramponing himself up between them into a laughing three-way hug.

'And who was that?' said Amy, wriggling away good-humouredly to set the bowls down on the scrubbed table. Benton swung the boy up onto a stool.

'Captain Winters, State Recruiting Committee,' said Benton, unconsciously catching the tone of the man's introduction. 'There's another rally, Saturday night, and they want me in on it. Special request, as it were.'

'From I know whom,' smiled Amy. Billyjim's hand made a dive for the bread. 'Not yet, my boy,' said his mother, holding him back as Benton cut in quickly with: 'For these and all Thy gifts we give Thee thanks, O Lord.'

Fine man, the bishop, mused Benton back in the drawing room after lunch, turning over the captain's phrase. Man of God, man of the world. How could that arm on his shoulder propelling him into that study be at once so friendly and so condescending? 'Now what is this all about, David? Can't have any funny business you know, not in the Anglican communion. And what exactly *were* you up to last Sunday? Something a little Irish, if my spies can be believed.' A week later Benton could still feel the sheer solidity of his presence, a kind of well-fed, well-washed quality. He could still see the slight rise and fall of the pectoral cross on its purple ground, the continuous curve of chest and belly beneath it.

'Well, bishop, I suppose I must have ... implied ... that the war is, well, more of the world than of the spirit. It's not as simple as we thought. It's a war of, well, politicians, generals, manufacturers.' Benton had hesitated at this point, but encouraged by having got so far, he'd suddenly looked Barker directly in the eye for the first time and added, almost petulantly, he realised now: 'It should be stopped.'

'Of course, my boy,' the bishop had conceded grandly. 'A consummation devoutly to be wished—and in the meantime?'

'Well, we could at least ...'

'You do remember,' Barker went on, his grandeur shading rapidly to irritation—an unexpectedly slow pupil, 'what happened in Belgium? It's all rather elementary, I suspect. Which do you prefer, the freedom of Britain or the tyranny of Prussia? There's not much doubt where the Christian path lies between those two, I think.'

'No ... but ...'

'Then you think it's none of our business, do you?' the bishop cut in again with a dexterity which, given his bulk, seemed almost shocking. Benton remembered now Winters' comment about football—and his own performances as scarecrow fullback in the school thirds. 'Twelve thousand miles and another world completely. You do remember German New Guinea, do you not? And the *Emden*?' It was like a feint or a fending-off on the rugby field. Benton could do nothing but scan the leather spines on the bookshelves: Cruden's *Concordance*, Crockford's *Clerical Dictionary* ... 'And how many weeks would Australia last—with the British Navy at the bottom of the sea?' Then with the hint of a smile, his urbanity returning: 'And we do belong to the Church of England, do we not, David?'

It had not gone well. Benton, respectful, uncertain still, outmanoeuvred from the start, dismissed like an erring schoolboy, had caught the Mail north that afternoon and as the rails clattered inexhaustibly beneath him saw the arguments lined up against him, neat, comprehensive, impenetrable. The bishop could probably summon up a dozen more at will.

And, yes, Benton had to admit that what few dissenting voices there were did sound a little weak with, well, their undertones of self-interest, impracticality, even cowardice. And yet, sitting here in his drawing room and occasionally looking up at bare trees through chequered glass, he could not find as he searched the fine leaves of his New Testament any trace of that grand presence or his maxims. The prayers of chaplains ascended on all sides; and God, it seemed, must give ear to them all—or none.

Late in the afternoon with his collar off he was scything the grass behind the house, the last cut perhaps before winter. He ran the whetstone along the blade, testing the edge against his thumb. The long sweeps were becoming expert now, and he'd begun to enjoy it: the way the prairie grass slumped neatly sideways, the new smell of it and the memories in the sweat itself of things he'd ten years since abandoned—the thicker smell of horsesweat, unsaddling in the dark after a day's mustering, the pleasurable ache in calves and thighs as you walked, foreshortened, through Paddy's Lucerne to a homestead light. Three of them there'd been out there at Wallagundah in the holidays from school, mustering together: older brother Lyall, still running the place now, his mind a dour labyrinth of stock and fences; younger brother Jack, the tearaway, the horseman of the three (though a bit impetuous with cattle) who'd enlisted last June, seen the end of Gallipoli and was now near Armentières somewhere; and David himself, in between, the only matriculant, destined since no-one could quite remember for the church.

It had not been a road to Damascus exactly—more something growing slowly from the chapel at school: alto in the choir, a server at Holy Communion, the thick sweet smell of wine on a winter morning, the voices at Evensong lifting hymns to the rafters, the words which to David gave up their meaning and were for others a distant reassurance (death was so far away, after all) or a reference point at most, the words which would

later lead him neatly across town to St John's Theological
College and onwards to ordination. Often at school he would
have preferred to conform more exactly to the hard-eyed but
easier ways around him, but the corridor jibes of 'Holy Joe' were
nothing ultimately to the symmetries of the Trinity, the endless
promise of redemption, the challenging black void (beginning
with a dormitory ceiling) into which one's prayers were offered
up. There'd been the subtle calibrations too of matching such
symmetries to the desolate yet busy four-part daily round—
meals and classroom, sport and sleep. Then, at the centre, the
figure of Christ himself with his unfailing compassion, his
absolute demands. Sometimes in these holiday musters he
felt a similar surrender as the cattle moved without volition
or stockwhip from larger to smaller paddocks, then down the
stock-route into town and their extinction.

Scything steadily among such memories, he drew near
the withered stems of Amy's last tomatoes, the yellowed fruit
caught and split by frost. Some men in his position might have
found a gardener, or at least have had the yardman extend his
attentions to the rectory, but David and Amy both preferred
things as they were. The light sweat he had now was part of some
wider satisfaction which included her warm and substantial
body in bed at night, the bedroom fire collapsing slowly in the
grate, the invisible breathing of Billyjim next-door. But working
with a scythe these days you never quite forgot ... Jack in France
somewhere, the brilliant 'cold steel' of the journalists. How had
that letter gone in the *Express* last year? *Our big lads lifted Turks
on the end of their bayonets and hurled them over their heads.*

**2**

'"For this my son was dead, and is alive again; he was lost and is found."' Even in this lesser context Benton seemed to savour the rhetoric, the sheer sound of the words. 'Any questions? Yes, Douglas.'

'Please, sir, do ministers or priests have to go to the war?' There was a light titter from some of the bigger ones.

'Well, Douglas, as you probably know, no-one is forced to join the army to fight overseas but there is compulsory training for home defence.' Benton smiled down at them irresolutely. 'Some of you older boys will soon be doing your Saturday drill, I expect.' A hand shot up.

'Sir, sir, my brother's already been doing that since Christmas.'

'My brother's already in the real army,' a small girl smirked. 'My mummy says he's somewhere in France right now.' Their tinny voices seemed to shatter on the walls, their fragility in this wooden room sometimes more than he could bear. Morning came in weakly through tall windows. Benton looked down from the dais.

'Well, Douglas, does that answer your question?'

'Not really, sir.' His face was thin and serious with no mischief in it. 'I was just wondering, you know, if ministers, people like yourself, if they have to go or not. Wouldn't seem right somehow.'

'Well, some do go as chaplains—to help the soldiers and the wounded but not to fight themselves.' This seemed to be near enough for Douglas but not for the little girl (what was her name? Steggart?) whose brother was 'somewhere in France'.

'Anyway, sir, my grandpa says it's not fair. Call 'em all up he says, no exceptions. Send 'em all over to help our Jimmy, that's what he says,' she parroted. 'Politicians, clergy, the lot. Send 'em all!' She might, Benton thought, with the scratchiness of her voice, have been a gramophone record. As if to lift the needle the bell outside rang suddenly three or four times on its pole. Slipping neatly into the short silence that followed, Benton said, 'And now, children, just before we go to play let us finish with the Lord's Prayer. Our Father, which art ...' And standing somehow aside from his automatic shaping of the words Benton found himself wondering again at the eternal primness of all the little Miss Rosemary Steggarts, and that different flat straightforwardness of boys, their minds wheeling and striving already in the dust outside.

When the children had all brushed past him Benton strolled up to join McPhee, the headmaster, and his two teachers in a small room, not much more than a storeroom, at the end of the veranda. There was an indeterminate smell of chalk, dried glue, old texts and now dark, stewed tea. McPhee, in his late forties, a large-boned, thoughtful man with sternly slicked-down hair, handed Benton his usual sour black cupful. 'Still no sugar, eh?' he said, ladling a couple of teaspoonfuls into his own. 'How are you finding 'em these days?' he asked in a tone meant to be heartier than it turned out to be (was Benton really a colleague or not?). 'Start to feel their oats a bit, some of those sixth graders. War's got 'em all stirred up one way or another.' Benton nodded across the top of his cup, noticing the way McPhee never quite did up the button of his collar and the light haze of chalkdust (dandruff?) on his shoulders. 'Twenty names already on the board out there. Three killed.'

'I know,' said Benton, having remembered as he'd come in the three separate clicks of three front gates and the three successive telegrams in his inside coat pocket. (*AND DESIRE TO CONVEY TO YOU THE PROFOUND SYMPATHY OF THE MINISTER ...*)

'Young Tommy Paget,' said McPhee, trailing off. Looking

out the door Benton saw, or thought he could see, the younger
Paget—Johnny?—skirmishing half-heartedly at the edge of a
group near the weathershed. He was always less than certain
with names.

'Makes you think, doesn't it,' said McPhee slowly. 'Younger
brothers of the younger brothers. And I don't call Gallipoli
much of a sign.' He reached for a large red folder topping a pile
of exercise books. 'Don't fancy the Germans'll prove any easier.'

'No,' agreed Benton distantly. 'Not for a time yet.'

McPhee had begun to look down at what Benton saw was
the school roll, its copperplate names, the daily Xs. Superfluous
suddenly, Benton made his farewells and nodded vaguely to
the other teachers (a young woman, and a man about McPhee's
age, fairly recent arrivals, neither of whose names he could
remember); then walked along the veranda and out through the
turnstile. There near the gate on two 3x2s was the *Roll of Honour,
Geradgery Public School*, in order of enlistment, together with
three small crosses. *For God, King and Country*, it said at the top.

Turning five minutes later into the main street, occupied at this
moment by sun and shadow only, Benton saw that Winters and
his sergeant had things well in hand. *Patriotic Rally*, it said in the
butcher's window to a background of mutton chops and sirloin.
*May 27, eight p.m., Geradgery School of Arts.*

*See the Picture Film 'Heroes of the Dardanelles'. Hear Captain
Winters, A.I.F., and Sergeant Dalby, late of Gallipoli. Introduced
by the Rev. D. Benton and Councillor Edward McLennan, Shire
President.*

*God Bless Daddy*, it said at the post office behind the fluted
sandstone pillars, *And Send Him Help. Follow Your Mates—Enlist*,
and a ship sailed west into a bloody sunset. *Australia Will Be
There*. The strut of the melody (that long-held, wavering central
vowel) sang through Benton's head as he remembered for a
moment those earlier days around the piano in the parish hall
with Mrs Giddins jabbing out the chords. Then, suddenly, as he

dawdled there by the post office steps, mesmerised perhaps by sunlight and silence, there was a voice.

'Morning, Mr Benton.' A youth was bounding down the steps in front of him. The sheer energy astonished him.

There was a newness in the face, Benton saw now, which suggested that shaving was not quite a daily necessity. 'Just about got my dad talked round. Should be gone by July anyway.'

'That's fine, Johnny,' said Benton. It was coming back to him now. Young Bartrim, a wall of groceries behind him, biscuits, starch, hardware. 'You sure he can do without you at the store?' The automatic question.

'Yeah, it's a woman's job anyway, counterjumping.' Benton looked at the brick wall of the post office. *The Call of Humanity*. 'See you on Saturday night then, sir.' Was it the anticipation of military training that made his deference so enthusiastic?

'Yes,' said Benton obliquely. 'I suppose so.' But the boy had vanished already into veranda shadow three doors away. Slowly Benton headed off in the same direction, studying Winters' posters all the way up the street ... the baker's, the saddler's, Bartrim's General Store. There was even one tied to the fence wire of the machinery yard across the street near Elder Smiths. And through the doors of both the Royal and the Hibernian he made out already a couple of early drinkers.

The sun was proving stronger than it looked and as he turned into Cardigan Street (one of the 'better' streets) Benton felt the sweat in the armpits of his singlet and the special dampness of celluloid collars. Mrs Giddins, too, had had something to do with it. 'Why don't you call on Mrs Buchanan? I'm sure it would make all the difference. I don't really see why she wouldn't want to help out.' He made a diagonal across the street and unlatched the gate of 31, a wide-verandaed house of brick, well set off the ground on granite. Mrs Buchanan ... He'd really only managed (had the courage) to call on her once since the telegram last

August. It had not been one of the easier ones. Her strangeness then had set a crack in him which had been widening, not quite noticed, ever since.

He struck twice with the tarnished knocker, heard it echo down the hall; then saw her gaining shape through the stained glass as she came to the door.

'Good morning, Mr Benton. Do come in.'

'Thank you, Mrs Buchanan. Just thought I'd ...

The flank of her face which he saw as she led him down between ferns and hallstand did not continue the finishing-school smile that had met him. In the living room something of the original returned and Benton, when she had asked him to sit down, spent a moment glancing around the room. The details of that first visit reaffirmed themselves: the four turning balls of the eight-day clock under its dome of glass, the madonna and child statuette, the small palm in its corner, watered but dusty.

'Tea?' said Mrs Buchanan, not moving from the sofa.

'No, thanks all the same. Just had some down at the school. Not as nice as yours though, if I remember,' he added, the sourness of McPhee's brew still on the roof of his mouth. She made no reply, not even the slight, self-deprecating chuckle which in Benton's kettle-filled rounds habitually followed this remark. Mrs Buchanan (Florence) just sat there and stared, the grey streaks in her hair untouched and emphasising, Benton thought, the handsomeness of that original from which this current face had come. Fifteen years older than Amy perhaps?

'How's it been going then? No problems with the girl?'

'No. She still comes three afternoons a week. Quite enough really. And old Mr Parkins looks after the garden, of course.'

'You haven't been indisposed then? It's just that we hadn't seen you at church and ...'

'No,' said Mrs Buchanan with a firmness which might have stopped some other man not under Mrs Giddins' pressure. It was a negation which seemed to embrace the whole of St Jude's and every aspect of its doings.

'And, well, Mrs Giddins—you remember her—was wondering if you might like to help with the Women's Guild. They're having a Patriotic Stall next Friday week and she thought ...'

'I'm sorry, Mr Benton, but I don't really think I'd be interested. I can't see that it ...' She stopped herself from going on.

Benton saw that he should be on his feet and going, but for some reason continued to sit there rubbing one distant shoe lightly against the other. It seemed to irritate her. He looked up at the small, steel-framed photograph of her son, a bemused but determined Light Horse private, on his first leave from training, still a little self-conscious under his hat and plume. There was a slash of black ribbon across the top right-hand corner. 'You know,' began Benton, 'you really must ...'

'I know that, Mr Benton. And, I suppose, I've tried. But I really can't see the point.' The expression she had worn down the hall stared at him now without disguise or apology. As his gaze ducked away from hers he ran over in his mind what little the town had managed to tell him about the Buchanans. Benton's talent for gossip was minimal; Amy's rather more but limited by circumstance. Father Dwyer, that fluent priest, undoubtedly knew more than both of them together. Even so there was an outline: young Nicky at his good Sydney school, bit of a misfit both there and at home, for five years more a trouble to his father who stolidly and reasonably refused him any real say on the place and died in that summer before the war, mother and son selling up as soon as he was underground and moving into town (not Sydney, as most had predicted) where, with capital in hand, Nicky had just begun to meditate his next move when 4 August arrived. For reasons gone with him at Gallipoli a year later, Nicky had caught the first train south. The sharpness of that original farewell as much as the eternity of the last was, Benton knew, the explanation of what stared through him now.

'Well, if there's anything I can do ...' he said, getting to his feet at last. The desire to be at the door seemed strong in both of them. 'Mustn't keep the wife waiting, I suppose. She does like to have lunch early, you know; catch little Billyjim at the strategic moment, as it were.' The heavy front door with its tinted panels had begun to swing. 'You will let me know if there's ...' As he looked back from the bottom of the steps, he saw that she had not yet moved from behind the door. Through the glass he saw her greenish, blurred head tip forward into her hands. Once more the gate clicked shut behind him.

'Daddy's home!' yelled Billyjim, running down the hall and casting himself on the air. His father took him like a passed football and swung him up before his face. 'How's my little Billyjimbo?' Benton kissed and nibbled the pure little wrinkle of his son's ear. How could this be the same flesh that had so troubled St Paul? Billyjim's was almost translucent, almost spirit anyway. Wriggling and reaching high for his father's thinning hair, the boy was borne away down to the kitchen. Amy was just setting down the bowls as they came in.

'Guess who came for morning tea?' Benton smiled slightly, hovering near the table. 'On his way to Glen Innes. Quite forgotten your Thursday class, of course.' They sat down, the soup steaming before them, thick and green. Benton went quickly into grace, his mind slipping sideways, even as he did so, towards a stained-glass blur.

'He's certainly a character in that car,' Amy went on. 'Had the curate with him but he still insists on driving himself. Young Henry twirls the crank and away they go. Maybe he's right with Henry's eyes the way they are.'

Benton smiled despite himself. He appreciated, even if he did not quite have it himself, Amy's taste for the absurd. The bishop there behind the high wheel as if in full regalia, the lean, bespectacled curate crouched over the handle fearing perhaps some sudden episcopal release of the clutch—there was something stilted, flickering, almost picture show about it,

or there was when Amy told it. 'And what did he really want ...
apart from a scone or two?'

'Just keeping an eye out, I suppose. You know him. The
Vigilant All-knowing Eye.' An owlish phrase Barker had been
known to use himself in jest, but to his ministers scattered
through New England it was serious enough. 'Oh, and he did
say he was depending on you on Saturday night. Not *quite* sure
what he meant by that.'

Benton said nothing, gazing abstractedly at Billyjim and
leaving his soup untouched. Called in on Mrs Buchanan, he was
about to say, but would not have known quite how to continue.
Billyjim grinned and dunked his bread.

## 3

'And now, ladies and gentlemen,' Winters was saying, thrusting himself into the screen's still-flickering acetylene white square while, at the same time, Sergeant Dalby set a match to a couple of lamps on either side of the stage, 'having seen the gallantry of which our men have already shown themselves capable only a year ago, we come to the real business of the evening, the call to arms.' It was clear Winters was trying to capitalise on the moment of adjustment and silence which might naturally follow the last few frames. But already there was a small, disappointing movement towards the door from several parts of the hall. The captain had to raise his voice a little, its English inflections becoming more marked. 'Allow me to introduce forthwith our chairman for this evening, a man who needs no introduction, Mr David Benton, vicar of Geradgery, a man who has supported the patriotic cause from its inception. The Reverend David Benton.'

'Where's young Dwyer, the Irish feller, then?' called a well-liquored voice from the back. 'Berlin or Dublin?' Benton, having mounted the stage, advanced towards the lectern, nervous and confident at once.

'Ladies and gentleman,' he began with an urbanity he did not feel, 'this is hardly a sectarian moment. Captain Winters, our regional recruiting officer, has asked me to chair proceedings tonight not so much as a clergyman of the Church of England, but as a man well known to most of you and a man, like you, sir, committed to the Allied cause.' The jibe, and Benton could only just believe he'd made it, brought some scattered applause and a number of heads and hats turned back towards the interjector. Benton stared for a moment into the audience and saw more clearly what he'd noticed earlier—women for the most part, and bald heads catching the light.

'It is the minister who, in his pastoral duties, comes to know the cost of war as well as any man. It is he who sees the widow bereft and the fatherless children—but it is he too who realises this is a fearful struggle, a fight to the death no less, between Prussian tyranny on the one hand and British democracy on the other.' He could feel, almost with relief, the rhetoric taking over, the delicate problem of truth being set aside by style. 'There is no doubt in my mind which of these two more closely approaches a truly Christian society,' he went on, realising as he did so the source of his phrases. 'The Empire did not seek this war, let us be clear on that, but now that the Kaiser has thrust it upon us there is only one path and that is through to victory. And the way to that, as our prime minister has made only too clear, is through the Big Battalions.'

'Three cheers for Billy!' came the voice again from the back. The first exodus had finished now.

'No-one pretends it will be a victory without sacrifice or for that matter a speedy one, and no-one, I imagine, has yet forgotten Mr Fisher's memorable promise of the last man and last shilling.' There was another more muffled round of applause, dampened perhaps by the gloves of women.

'Let's hope it don't come to that,' said a new and quite sober voice. 'There'll be a Chinaman or two about then, that's for sure.'

'Or a townful of kanakas,' said a voice next to it, a man's voice thick with disdain.

'And what about the money part?' came another voice from beside the first. They were all a group, Benton saw, as he tried to accustom himself to being interrupted. 'What about old Billy Phillips? He's hardly down to his last shilling. Or Nathan Jackson, if it comes to that. It's still pretty good in the wool trade.'

'Shame!' cried an old lady, leaping fraily to her feet and turning on them. 'Don't you remember Lieutenant Phillips who died at Gallipoli—and Leo Jackson? And shirkers like you have the gall to show yourselves in public!'

'Ladies and gentlemen,' called Benton at last, reaching perhaps a little too hard for that authority which came so easily at St Jude's, 'let us not profane the memories of those who have made the supreme sacrifice; let us turn to the business at hand. As your chairman I should now like to introduce Councillor Edward McLennan, president of Geradgery shire, a man well known to you all and a man, I might say, with three sons currently serving in the A.I.F.'

McLennan got up from where he'd been sitting off to one side, strikingly backdropped by a Union Jack—a spreading, resilient man of sixty or so who took his time in reaching the lectern. 'Ladies and gentlemen,' he began easily, 'apart from one or two disaffected or, should I say, infected elements, I'm sure we're all agreed that this war is the greatest crisis which has so far faced our young nation.' Captain Winters, sitting stiffly in his chair beside Benton, gave the vicar one long, doubtful stare then looked away sternly towards the lectern. The 'fatherless children', Benton saw, was cutting it a little fine. '... for make no mistake,' McLennan was saying, 'that's just what these men have done—they've put us on the map and I'm a proud man indeed to have three sons among them.' There was a dutiful ripple of applause. 'Which rather brings me to my point. Who can doubt that in the coming months the need will become more and more desperate? We need a multitude more men and we need them now.' McLennan paused, a long, chairman's silence. Benton, innocently assuming him finished, rose to acquit his chairman's role but McLennan, ignoring him entirely, glanced suddenly over his right shoulder at Winters. 'So here to tell you how many men and what kind, and all the latest military intelligence, is that notable veteran of the South African war, our district recruiting officer, Captain Winters.'

Winters, his face alert and shining in the gaslight, was already at the lectern as McLennan resumed his chair amid considerable applause and a few shouts of 'Good on you, Ned!'

Benton, back in his seat but still embarrassed, looked once at Winters ('every inch an officer', as he saw the women thinking) and began a study of the first row. Not an unfamiliar angle, looking down like this, but remarkable how as a speaker one always addressed the mass and only as an observer did one attempt the particular. A paradox, he knew, like that of the publicly articulate and privately silent man he knew himself to be. Everything was so much easier from pulpit or platform. It was the particulars, always, which resisted. Mrs Buchanan, for instance. And there, to take one more example, was Mrs McGill with her husband, Bill, who never actually came to church but walked his wife right up to the gate, then strolled back down to the park (or was it Norton's Café) till twelve, when he would return to take up again his Phyllis's arm and walk home. 'A Darwinist,' Mrs Giddins had declared, a decision which, like all her others, was best left unchallenged. 'Fairy tales for grown ups' was the common report of McGill's theological views. Though Phyllis, for all Mrs Giddins' not so subtle pressure, had never joined the Guild (that might perhaps have been pressing Bill too far), their views at this moment, Benton saw, looked close enough. Their second son, Frank, was 'somewhere in France'; their attention to Winters' flow of words undivided.

'Yes,' the captain was conceding now, gripping the lectern with both hands and leaning down confidentially, 'there was a time when this was an emotional issue, a time when men rushed to the colours, eager to do their duty for Country, King and Empire before the excitement was over. At this point, alas, we know rather better. No, ladies and gentlemen, I do not present you with rhetoric, I present you with facts.'

What these were Benton did not quite absorb. He was staring again down into the first few rows—a little depressed, even with the inadequate light, at how many faces he failed to recognise. 'More Presbyterian than Anglican, I'm afraid,' he remembered the bishop saying when he'd taken up the parish five years before. One unknown in particular held him: a youth, eighteen perhaps, his face a pale, drawn surface beneath which currents shivered obscurely. The mother was there beside him, tight-lipped and upright. '… young men, eighteen to forty-five years, single or widowers without children, five foot six in height, chest expansion thirty-three inches …' It was a formula, Benton saw, which measured the youth exactly. His face seemed to buckle at Winters' words as if under an almost barometric pressure.

'There are those who say Australia has done enough, that New South Wales has done enough, that Geradgery has done enough.' The words, like their author, had a nervous shimmer of their own which, if interrupted, might cause them to vanish entirely. Though Amy, by necessity and preference, was at home, Benton could almost see her sceptically lifted eyebrows beside him. 'Australia's contribution is still far less than Britain's; New South Wales, the most populous state, is only just ahead of Victoria—and Geradgery, ladies and gentlemen, I'm reliably informed, is still the home of several score of eligibles who in England would already have been compelled to offer their services. Undoubtedly they have their reasons for holding back and quite honourable, I imagine, many of them are, but how telling can they be when the Allied plight is fully known, as I have made it known to you tonight.' There was a sudden, expert drop in tone. 'I wonder how well these footballers, these billiards players, will sleep tonight when they hear their comrades' call coming faintly, but clearly nevertheless, all those twelve thousand miles from France? How well will they sleep? That's what I ask you. How well will they sleep?' The last words were left to hang in the air. Benton again got up on his feet and was again forestalled. 'And now,' said the captain somewhat triumphantly into the silence he had created and catching Benton halfway across the stage, 'let me present you tonight with one of Australia's unsung but genuine heroes, Sergeant Athol Dalby, late of Gallipoli, who but for the wounds he received there would be in France this very moment.'

The sergeant, not so kempt as Winters, stepped forward with a slight limp to the lectern and paused a good fifteen seconds before starting, his toughened, sallow face in the lamplight a contrast to the gloss of Winters'. Why was it, Benton wondered as he sat down again, that an officer's uniform must fit so exactly and the other ranks' scarcely at all? The misfit in Dalby's case was not degrading, however. It seemed to emphasise the residual and only slightly reduced strength within it. Dalby spoke more softly than his captain but just as audibly. There was no 'Ladies and gentlemen'.

'Unlike most of you, I guess, I've been there.' Benton saw Winters' face beside him give an almost nervous tic. 'I can't pretend it's an easy life. It's dirty and it's dangerous but it's got to be done and the more people prepared to do it the easier it'll be all round. Though it's true to say you won't find a better mob of blokes than you get in the A.I.F. Bit rough, some of them, cooling their heels in Egypt, as you might have heard, but they come through when needed, make no mistake about that.' Dalby stopped a moment and peered into the shadows before him, as if to confirm some earlier surmise. Only the first few rows were distinguishable. 'People often ask me what it was like. Well, that's impossible to say. If you've been there you know and if you haven't there's no-one who can ever tell you. So if you ask me what I'm doing up here then I guess I'd just say I'm helping out me mates as best I can. Jacko Turk has got me skittled in the knee but that doesn't stop me from rounding up a bit of help against Fritz. Force of numbers is the only thing that'll work in the long run, I reckon.' He stopped again but not deliberately this time. It was as if a page had got lost somewhere. 'So,' Dalby rapidly concluded on a different level altogether, 'if you're a tough young feller of five foot six or more and a chest of 33 inches just give us your name at the end of the show and we'll take it from there.'

'Thank you, sergeant,' said Winters, stepping forward into the loudest applause by far of the evening. 'One of our genuine

"Heroes of the Dardanelles",' he added over the clapping which at length he had to silence with a raised hand. He turned to Benton who'd found himself applauding as warmly as anyone. 'And now, if Mr Benton's agreeable, I'll ask him to lead us in a short prayer before the singing of "God Save the King".' This too was undiscussed and impromptu, a special touch that Winters might or might not retain for future use. Benton came forward, not quite surprised, and after a suitable hesitation to let the mood secure itself, began to improvise, competently enough, but more, he realised increasingly, like a chairman summarising discussion than a man of God leading his flock beyond the physical.

'O Lord God, send us and all who rule over us Thy guidance in this our hour of need. Send Thy blessings on all those of our countrymen who are striving in our war for Christian values and make us worthy, O Lord, of their sacrifice.' The words, Benton realised as he uttered them, might just as well be Barker's. He could see without looking Winters' nod of satisfaction behind him. Another, more personal, direction seemed to offer itself. 'Send, too, Thy comfort to those bereaved, the wives without husbands, the children without fathers, and send Thy guidance to those who would question our struggle and let them see where justice lies. We pray, too, for our enemies, that they may abandon the error they have chosen and return to the better instincts of their race. We pray, also, Lord, for those who tonight will make the decision to serve their country in His Majesty's forces. For Thine is the Kingdom, the Power and the Glory, for ever and ever, Amen.'

At which Mrs Giddins, candlelit at the piano, struck the premonitory chord. The audience rose to its feet and launched successfully into the national anthem. Captain Winters, who clearly had a fine voice, led on into the second stanza but few, including Sergeant Dalby, were able to follow him there, thus forcing him and Mrs Giddins to take it manfully through as a kind of duet. Mrs Giddins, down there below in front of the

stage and off to one side, was, Benton saw, a little impatient with
the silence behind her but far from embarrassed. This for her
could well be, given the captain's stainless bearing, a moment
to remember.

As two more lamps were lit at the back of the hall and the
official party on stage (apart from Benton and, in another
way, Dalby) provisionally congratulated itself, the audience
dispersed with stunning swiftness through the door. Benton,
almost nauseous, turned aside from McLennan and Winters
and saw with surprise (it was almost as though he'd forgotten
the purpose of the meeting) the pale, anonymous youth and his
mother waiting to be noticed in front of the stage. Apart from
them, and Mrs Giddins impatiently striking a dead note on the
piano, the body of the hall was empty.

# 4

A week on from the rally winter had closed in completely. June days scudded low overhead driven by sleet, or otherwise began with frost and cleared to watery light—at its best, Benton noticed, among the stiffened elms and birches of the park and church grounds. The war arrived by paper as always—the Armidale *Express* twice weekly and the day-late Sydney *Herald*. The A.I.F. (complete with young Jack) was scrapping and raiding in the Armentières sector; the Germans and French were draining each other at Verdun still, and word of the 'big push' to relieve it was filtering through the news reports. Beatty's success by sea at Jutland and Brusilov's thrust in the Carpathians seemed almost to console for the vanishing of Kitchener, gone down bravely with his ship off the Orkneys. Reading the splendid elaborations on official communiqués and the occasional bluff letter from the Front while pulled up at the drawing room fire, Benton sensed, but knew he could not know, what lay behind them. The letters, courtesy a patriotic father, were vivid enough, even brutal; the occasional washed-out photographs of broken villages, stripped fields and forests were factual too, but somewhere through and beyond them he was beginning to distinguish, if only in the shadows of his reluctant imagination, something more shocking, more infernal.

Jack's letters from those last months at Gallipoli had been no less hearty than the ones in the newspapers. They had come no doubt from another world but used as a courtesy the language of the addressee—no point in giving his mother more to worry about than she had already. *We're giving old Jacko as good as we get, or better, but it looks like things are quietening down a bit now. They say that on the first day they got to the top and saw the straits on the other side but no-one's been there since. Old Nipper Barton's over here, you might remember him, used to work over at Scotty's place. Frank Webster too, he's in the same section, came in with reinforcements last week. Nicky Buchanan's gone though. Turned out a good soldier they say. Got right through the landing and the Lone Pine business. Not so good for his mother. First the flies and now the winter coming on—might be even colder than Geradgery! And don't worry too much, Mum. I must be one of the lucky ones.*

The letters were invariably for Violet, their mother, never for David or for Lyall. Each one, Benton saw, gave her one more reprieve (at least he was alive six weeks ago and if anything had happened since there'd have been a telegram). David though, sitting across from his mother in the living room at Wallagundah after those Saturday lunches every six weeks or so, had never quite been able to focus on them. The world the letters came from in their scrappy hand kept slipping away leaving just the three of them: Lyall outside somewhere doing some small job that couldn't wait (sitting in drawing rooms was clergymen's business after all); Violet, mother of all three and in her fifties now, bird-like on the sofa, thin but unstooped; and David himself, more remote in a way than Amy and Billyjim who would be outside there walking among the apple trees, flowering, fruited or bare with the season. It was not so much that Jack really had anything against him. It was more that Jack simply found it impossible to deal with anyone who took God seriously. Jack's departure last year, added to David's much earlier one into the church, had somehow thinned the distance between them and made it absolute.

Since the sermon back in early May when the first edges of his doubts had discovered themselves, and since the reprimand which had followed, Benton had stuck to his gospel for the day and let the war attend to itself. The rally had been difficult, embarrassing even, but back in St Jude's and in its weekly expectations there was a continuity which took one forward regardless. Three more deaths there'd been since then, three more golden crosses on the Honour Roll down at the school and one more on the roll which the Parish Council had put up in the vestibule of its church.

The telegram in this last case had not been too difficult—its address a small wooden cottage on the other side of the railway already weighed down by so much ill-chance as to make this only the current example. They were not a family who came to church often: the mother, three times a year, drafted the whole family out as if to hold onto certain decencies which might otherwise slip away altogether. The father (a fettler, if Benton remembered correctly) had read the vicar's face at once and held out his hand for the envelope; a rough, outdoor hand which did not invite a shake of condolence. Benton, speaking his few clumsy words, would almost have preferred resentment. But instead the man spoke softly his thanks and not impolitely shut the door in Benton's face. Walking back across town in the reddening cold light of the winter evening and under the viaduct, Benton winced from the stare of old men in doorways and their suddenly stilled grandchildren, curious in the streets. They all seemed to know what he'd been at and did not separate him from it, no less a part of the process than the nameless German sniper who'd begun it.

So as June wore away into July and Captain Winters, it was learned, had gone back to Sydney to consolidate strategy, Benton did nothing further. Propriety and continuity renewed themselves endlessly. But in his prayers and meditations certain texts began increasingly to hang awry. *Jesus answered, My Kingdom is not of this world; if my kingdom were of this world, then would my servants fight, that I should not be delivered to the Jews; but now is my kingdom not from hence.* And then again those impossibilities in St Luke: *But I say unto you which hear, Love your enemies, do good to them which hate you ... And unto him that smites one cheek offer him also the other. Forgive and ye shall be forgiven.*

His own Christ, Benton saw now, had slipped back by

stages to not much more than a matter of ceremony and good sense, a figure who looked down with approval at the worthy asceticism of frosty communions, a figure who helped men towards considerate and careful lives. Now, for the first time in his readings, Benton began to feel the grit in the sandals, the single-minded ferocity of the original twelve, the rocky absolutes of His teaching. Without his really having spoken of it yet, Amy too seemed to have sensed the gap between what her husband had been declaiming and what emerged from the gospels when looked at closely. It was a realisation which, more each day for both of them, seemed to slip between the lines of newspapers, subtly shading as they read.

'Listen to this bit,' Amy had said one night late as they sat in front of the drawing room fire. She began to quote that morning's *Express*. 'The day for dependence on the high-minded volunteers, incomparable though they were, is past. Other more equitable and compelling means must be sought.' Benton stared down into the flames. She skipped a couple of paragraphs in which the 'means' were never quite described and went on, lightly mocking its hyperbole of tone: 'In the spirit of Christianity, in the cause of civilisation, of liberty and humanity; in the name of mankind and in the sight of God, now and forever, we must win the war.'

'Might have written that myself a couple of months ago,' said Benton with a difficult smile as she put down the paper.

'Chapter and verse?' inquired Amy, lifting an eyebrow.

'Christ and the moneychangers, maybe,' said David. 'Don't know what else. Though if we believe what we read the Germans have been up to more than changing money in Belgium.'

'Gallant little Belgium,' said Amy. In her own way, Benton could see now, Amy had been more than a little sceptical right from the outset. She it had been who'd jogged his memory on that Congo exposé some years back—the Belgian king's own personal colony, natives in chains and their hands cut off. The soldiers from her grandfather's Saxony would be of average brutality, she knew, but not quite the baby-impalers conjured in London.

In that August two years back and pregnant with Billyjim, Amy, like her husband, had been content enough with the papers' line but never, it was clear now, quite as swept up as David in the general concurrence, the popular surge. Benton could still locate in his stomach that June to August feeling, watching day by day the fragments clumsily but inevitably fitting together in a cartographic puzzle where every country consented to be a piece but none, it seemed, could control the game. Britain, it was curious to remember now, had stood off to the last, a British squadron attending the reopening of the widened Kiel canal only weeks before. And yet on 4 August the last fretted piece had slotted neatly into place. And so, along with all the rest, Benton had preached the Union Jack that Sunday.

Amy might have her doubts now but she too had done her share of patriotic work. It came, like everything else, with the job. Generally she made do with knitting. Mrs Giddins, friendly but insistent at the back door, had implied that a minister's wife might do a little more to help with recruiting and had passed her some literature. Benton remembered Amy's smile as she'd handed it on to him. *The recruiting committee*, Benton had read, *is of the opinion that the uplifting influence of the fair sex can be utilised in a novel manner to secure the enlistment of the eligible men of the state during the present crisis.* A medallion was available, it appeared, engraved with a quotation in French: '*QUI S'EXCUSE S'ACCUSE*'. Eligibles who inquired as to why the lady was wearing it, or its meaning, would be given it as a keepsake upon their enlistment. *There is no woman who would not rather suffer suspense and poverty for a hero than live in comfort with a coward.* The last phrase, novelettish though it was, rested alliteratively enough in the mind, but from the way Amy abutted so agreeably against his skinny frame in bed these winter nights, Benton knew there'd been no change, that she'd not seen it the way she might have. Cowardice though had its different orders. For two years one of them, despite the clerical exemption, had intermittently disturbed him, a kind that Winters and Barker would equally understand. Now it was another which would keep him an hour or more awake. Watching Amy asleep as he lay there staring at the ceiling or propped on his elbow, Benton was comforted by her amplitude of shape and spirit. The reassurance of God, for all his prayers, was that much further off.

## 5

Though St Jude's farewell to Johnny Bartrim, 'ex-counterjumper' (as he had it), was no different from all those which had preceded it, Benton was distinctly more disquieted. There was an extra focus to it somehow, being as it was on the Friday evening after news of the A.I.F.'s first showing at Fromelles came through but before the casualty lists of the following week. Now, as Johnny had foretold on the post office steps two months ago, parental permission and the requisite years had come through at last and he was away. The church send-off here in the parish hall would be just one of several. Thirty or so people took their seats, scraping them a little self-consciously on the hardwood floor.

'Ladies and gentlemen,' said Benton to get things under way. 'Fellow parishioners,' he added more democratically, 'we are gathered together here tonight informally for a very special purpose. Mr Johnny Bartrim is a young man well known to you all, and indeed to the whole Geradgery community—and especially, I may say, to the tennis players. I don't imagine any of you fortunate enough to see him in the grand final last month against the Presbyterians will readily forget it.' He paused and looked out over the small assembly: relatives, friends, a few church stalwarts, Mrs Giddins, of course, who had lit the lamps and somehow contrived even in July a small bowl of flowers on the table out the front. 'As you know,' Benton went on, finishing his survey with a glance at the boy's parents in the front row, Johnny comes from a very respected Geradgery family and I'm particularly pleased to welcome here tonight Mr and Mrs Bartrim in what must be for them a very proud, yet difficult, moment.' He looked down at the couple's front-row faces as if to check on what he'd said. In the linseed gloom of his general store Bartrim moved with much professional good humour but here, Benton saw, he was outside his expertise, as quiet and vulnerable as anyone else. The wife (Emma?), a wide foreshadowing of Amy and perhaps forty-five, Benton had seen more often in church than in the store where her absence from behind the counter was taken as an index of Bartrim's success.

'Hear, hear,' said an older voice and there was a light, polite clatter of applause. Illogically Benton thought of his own Billyjim (that fragile forearm on a grey blanket) and noted Johnny's fiercely slicked-down hair. It suggested a rather too rapid accession to responsibility. The exuberance seen in that encounter two months back was still there, but masked now by a new seriousness. Benton remembered the exact combination from 1914—so many similar expressions unfleshed in Shrapnel Valley.

'Johnny Bartrim is a young man who sees his duty with an unusual clarity and is therefore leaving this weekend for Holsworthy camp and thence for France.' It was a clarity, Benton realised, that he would have liked for himself—though not its consequence. Courage, too, had its different orders. 'I'm sure I speak for everyone here when I say that our most devoted prayers and sincerest good wishes go with him.' He bowed slightly, but not ironically, in Johnny's direction. 'And I'm sure there are several others who will want to second these remarks.'

'Yes, indeed, Mr Benton,' came a voice from down near the door, almost filling the hall. It was McPhee, the headmaster, who must have slipped in late and sat by himself in the last row of chairs. He was getting to his feet now. Benton pictured the chalk dust on his collar, the stewed black tea. 'I'm not perhaps the most frequent member of this congregation but I would like this opportunity to say that young Bartrim is one of the most decent young fellows we've ever had through Geradgery School. Though it's four years since he left he's still very much remembered there—and will be for some time to come—as a boy outstanding on the sportsfield and in the classroom and a pleasure to teach.' McPhee stopped but did not sit down. He seemed to feel this was not quite enough, or not quite what he'd intended to say anyway. Suddenly, with fierce conviction, as if almost a release, he added: 'And I for one feel sure that any cause which is served by young men such as Johnny Bartrim is not only morally just but certain to succeed, whether it be in one year or ten.' Benton, watching the audience, could feel the unspeakable time scale sinking in. McPhee's conviction seemed to be a handrail along the edge of an abyss. 'Though I for one, like you all, wish him a speedy and a safe return.'

Even as the headmaster finished Benton was still getting used to the idea of his being there at all. It was more than a year since he'd been to church and at the thirty or so earlier send-offs, many of them for ex-pupils, McPhee had hardly ever appeared, let alone spoken. His dark, slightly shambling presence was at once heartwarming—and, in a way, ominous.

Next on his feet was Tom Dalloway, a seventeen year old from the tennis club. He too had a short, two-sentence speech, predictable in every detail. Then, about to sit down, he suddenly leapt up again and added: 'And I reckon you'll be giving Fritz quite a hiding before you're through, too—just like the ones you gave most of us. We won't be forgetting those in a hurry.' He stepped round the end of the front row and extended his hand. 'All the best, Johnno.'

The choirmaster (Cyril Somerton) and the Women's Guild (Mrs Giddins) followed briefly in more formal vein. Johnny had spent some time in the choir—and Mrs Giddins (given Mrs Bartrim's contribution to the Guild) was not to be denied. Then, still a little puzzled by McPhee, Benton brought things to a close. 'And now if Johnny would kindly step forward I'll call upon Miss Ida Turnbull of our Girls Friendly Society to make a small presentation on behalf of us all here tonight.' Ida Turnbull was one of several girls who had waited, handkerchief in fist, for Johnny to make the hoped-for diagonal at dances in this very hall. And once or twice she might have been walked home had it not been for an edgy father hovering at the door. Benton, an awkward man himself in so many ways (though not on his feet before a crowd), ached for her confusion and was stirred by the way she overcame it, reaching for the gravity, even the poignance, she knew the occasion demanded. Her short, rehearsed list of standard phrases ('a small token of our esteem') was exactly fitting. Johnny, standing beside her out the front, accepted the small package and the light kiss that went with it and with a suitable blush turned to his audience, the first few rows. 'Thank you, Ida ... and thank you everyone. I'm not much of a speechifier, I guess, but I would just like to thank you all—and especially my parents, for all they've done—and I hope, like you, that all our prayers are answered and that, God willing, I'll soon be back here safe and sound. Thank you.'

As a short, impassioned burst of clapping rattled round the hall Benton caught himself unworthily noting the accuracy of Johnny's claim not to be a 'speechifier'. So many things were more important. A clergyman lived essentially in language, others in action. 'C'mon, open it,' someone called. Johnny, still a little flushed, respectfully stripped away the paper and held up a blue fountain pen. 'Genuine Onoto,' chirped someone as people began to crowd around to make their personal goodbyes. 'And make sure you use it.'

'The pen is mightier than the sword,' cracked Tom Dalloway.

## 6

As July ended and Pozières began to replace Fromelles in the news, the casualty lists declared more strongly what the headlines left out. Benton, habitually working his way down the *Herald*'s long alphabetical columns, grew more and more restless. By some chance it was Cyril Somerton rather than Amy who caught the force of it first.

'Well, looks like our boys haven't lost the Gallipoli touch, eh, Mr Benton?' Somerton suggested one cold Wednesday night as Benton was helping him lock up after choir. He looked down at Benton through rimless glasses, the autodidact seeking word from an expert—or one who ought to be. Benton, as Somerton spoke, was slipping a bolt home low on the front door, the wind outside howling to get in. 'Though it does look a bit on the costly side.' Benton stood up and looked directly at the parish honour roll, its golden names and unfilled spaces. Somerton, one of the Parish Council who'd set it there, was the newsagent and stationer and took an hour each morning over the *Herald*. 'I'm not sure about that Haig, though. Very determined, you have to give him that, but not the man Kitchener was—or Roberts, for that matter.' Benton still said nothing. Only thirteen at the time, he remembered the South African war rather vaguely, a kind of tin soldier war, garnished by exploits. Somerton apparently, two decades older, had followed the conflict in detail, or as much detail as the *Herald* and the *Illustrated London News* would permit. In the first days of 1914 it had given him a certain short-lived expertise, Benton had noticed, in after-church discussion. The choirmaster worked on in a slightly injured silence, straightening hymn books. At last the two men stood by the vestry door ready to go.

'Maybe they're all the same anyway,' said Benton abruptly.

'Beg your pardon?'

'I said they're all the same.' Benton looked now directly into the increasingly stunned plate of Somerton's face. 'What do they know with their maps and pointers back at H.Q.? What do we know, for that matter? Only what the newspapers choose to tell us. And how do the German papers have it, I wonder?' Benton was surprising himself as much as Somerton whom, in a way, he was no longer addressing. 'Vital Salient Holds Off Doomed Colonial Assault. Britain's colonial troops today were cut to pieces, wave after wave, by our stalwart Bavarian machine gunners.'

'It's a testing time, Mr Benton, as I remember you yourself saying.' Somerton looked shocked but even so rather pleased with his memory. 'How did it go now? "In the midst of suffering we begin to see what are the things that really matter".'

'Still true,' said Benton, 'just not quite in the way I meant it.' A new acidity had leaked into the minister's tone, making the choirmaster physically uncomfortable. 'Quite a vision, eh? All the young men, shoulder to shoulder, the nation united behind them, purified by self-denial, the hotels deserted, the bookmakers bankrupt.'

Somerton looked pained—a conductor who hears a flat voice somewhere. 'There are always quite a few at the Hibernian, I notice—even at this time of night. The shutters are up, of course, but you can hear them just the same. Quite a few young fellows too, I don't doubt.'

Benton, about to put out the last lamp, found himself looking instead at this older man whom he'd so far taken for granted—a small, reliable man who, in his foursquare way, obtained the best from his materials, patchy though they were these days. He saw that behind those little glasses his choirmaster was at something of a loss—even frightened. The professional, if slightly awkward, compassion that Somerton normally saw on his vicar's face had gone and there was nothing, or nothing which Somerton could yet accept, to replace it.

'Well, that's it then,' he said, opening the small side door as
Benton put out the final lamp. The sky as they faced it was cold
and black, scattered with windy stars and matched in a kind
of diminished reversal by the few scattered lights of the town
which lay a little below them. Benton stepped out first and they
parted without further words: Somerton heading stockily off
downhill into the wind and Benton almost blown across the
churchyard past bare trees to his vicarage door.

*Dear David*, ran the afternoon's letter. Benton stood with his
back to the drawing room fire. Stronger gusts now were blowing
a little smoke back down the chimney and into the room.
Amy was in an armchair knitting her khaki socks, her weekly
quota for the Women's Guild, three pairs—Mrs Giddins would
condone no fewer.

*I wonder if you'd care to sign the enclosed statement. We're aiming
for at least two or three ministers from all the major churches and
then to send it to the* Herald *and the* Argus.

*It's a pity we haven't caught up with each other since the old
days at St John's but I suspect I'm right in thinking you too might
have had enough of the worldly opportunism which passes these
days for patriotism among our leading churchmen. Did you see
Murdoch's book* The Laughter and the Tears of God *last year?
'We are fighting to make room for the Christian virtues—humility,
compassion, helpfulness, peace.' Do you see them in any greater
evidence these days? As you see, P.J. Reedy, Arthur Redlands and
Peter Crestwick have put their names to it already and I am hopeful
of getting support from some Roman Catholics in Melbourne and
a few of the Presbyterians. There is a time, you know, when not to
speak is to give assent.*

*Yours in Christ*
*Jeremy Frizelle*

Though Benton had not seen Frizelle in six or seven years he did recall at a synod hearing of Frizelle's having given up the ministry (no scandal to speak of ) and going into teaching. Certainly he could still picture him in a few selected situations: gravely eating his porridge in the college dining hall; his clean, intense face as he exercised with dumbbells and parallel bars in what had passed for the college gymnasium; and in the common room sometimes, his extraordinary doggedness in argument. There'd been a debate, Benton recalled now, for which Frizelle had been conscripted at the last minute. The tone of these after-dinner affairs had normally been light and ingenious, a kind of parlour game. 'You can't make an omelette without breaking eggs.' While the first three speakers had cleverly fooled with ends and means and made knowing allusions to the recent Russian duma, Frizelle, as second speaker for the opposition, had launched in with a totally serious and immaculate argument against capital punishment which, in its almost autistic remoteness, had effectively lost his team the debate. Benton could still remember the atmosphere of the common room, compounded equally of embarrassment and admiration. Frizelle had not smiled the whole evening.

*P.S.*, he'd added, *I'm enclosing the first draft of a pamphlet I'm working on. It may help to make up your mind.* Benton sat down now, feeling the warmth from the fire in the seat of his pants. He took up the five or so pages of carbon type again, phrases from which had been running through his head since lunch.

*If only the churches could unite with one voice to confront this infamy instead of consenting to it and abetting the materialist hysteria of the politicians, then might we see some moves for peace. Why must a fight be fought to the finish?*

It was coming back to him even more clearly now—the thick red embers of that common room fire into which he'd stared as Frizelle had gone on past the bell, gripped by the purity of his argument, the need to reach the Q.E.D. There was the unshakeable seriousness of the man too, the way he hated to be called 'Frizzle' on the tennis court.

*Let us for the moment consider the unthinkable—which, for those familiar with the Christian mysteries, should not be so very unusual. Let us imagine that a whole country, having thoroughly understood what Christ meant, decided unilaterally to disarm, melt down all its weaponry to scrap, and declare that henceforth it had done with war. Would their neighbours, as the worldly say, swoop down next day and destroy them? Might they not take some pause for wonder before hacking them to pieces and, having paused, reflect a little longer?*

Benton wondered about Frizelle's defection, how or why this man had come to abandon what he himself was still a part of. Not lack of conviction, evidently. The compromises, the small hypocrisies, perhaps, which got one through the day? The gap which so much depressed Benton now between what Christ had done and said two thousand years before and what his latter-day disciples could manage in 1916?

*Or let us assume,* Frizelle went on, *they took no pause and swept down nevertheless—would that be the end of God's purpose? Did not our very own faith grow and spread under one of the world's largest and cruellest tyrannies? Were not the slaves of this regime among our first converts? 'Render unto Caesar,' says Christ, 'the things which are Caesar's'—coinage, not our souls. The flag today has replaced the cross and the purity of our teaching has become instead a vehicle for the recruiting officer who deludes the young man into offering up his life not to God but to Mammon.*

A sudden knot went off in the fire, a kind of punctuation. David put the foolscap down, got up and stooped to poke at the fire. Amy blinked the strain out of her eyes and smiled at her husband's less than dextrous efforts with the poker. The big black kettle in the fireplace had boiled at last. She slipped away down to the kitchen to set up supper. Benton stood a while longer, his back to the fire; then sat down again to reconsider the statement itself.

*A Call to Peace,* it began. *We, the undersigned Christian ministers reject the current equation of Christianity and patriotism being made by so many of our colleagues. We do not believe that either side in this war can win, or claim, God's approval other than by doing its utmost for an immediate peace. With this in mind we call upon the Prime Minister to prepare a compromise proposal which can be presented to the several Allied heads of government and, through the good offices of President Wilson of the United States, be passed on also to Germany and its allies as the territorial basis for an immediate armistice. As an earnest of Australia's sincerity we ask that further recruitment cease forthwith and that Australian troops be withdrawn from all fronts as soon as practicable.*

It was the last sentence that turned him cold; the coldness he could still remember from Wallagundah when, just eleven, he'd gone out after rabbits with that old Martini-Henry he didn't quite know how to handle yet and, stumbling along a gully's edge, had almost blown the side of his head off: that same concussion in the ear. To Benton at this stage the idea of an immediate withdrawal was both absurdly logical—and more than a little cowardly. Though the bishop, he knew, on seeing Benton's signature underneath, would hardly have the same ambivalence. Those rows of leather-bound theology, the low chair as Barker loomed above him. There was no doubting the consequences.

'That last sentence is the problem, I suspect?' said Amy, back now and pouring the tea. 'It's no wonder he's only got three signatures. And he's not even in a position to sign it himself, you say.'

'And yet,' said David, 'without that there's nothing—just the pacifist piety to match the patriotic one.'

'He'll hardly be asking His Lordship for a signature, I imagine. You're not really thinking of signing?' She was sitting beside him now, her warm, substantial presence in itself urging practicality. There was no lifted eyebrow now.

'I don't know,' said Benton, standing up with his cup and saucer and moving in front of the fire. 'Why don't you just head off to bed? I won't be long. Might just take a bit of a walk.' Amy

half-smiled across at him. There was no way you'd find her out
in that wind. David, she'd long observed, liked to cast himself
upon it, as if diving into another medium. It had a way of sorting
things out—'blowing things into place', as he'd said more than
once.

Hands thrust down in pockets and leaning into the north wind
which swept from a snowfall higher up, Benton strode his
moonless gravel circuit and each time noted a last few plane
leaves flapping near the street lamp on the corner near the
church, the flame flickering but never quite going out. The stars,
to his wind-watered eyes, seemed to shift in and out of focus,
offering only distances, relative at first then absolute. The God
out there? The God within? Either way the killing went on—the
boys of '87, the boys of '92. What was it now? List 203? The lists
were herds of Gadarene swine, filled up with another's madness.
And Jack among them, a corporal now, for whom (unlike his
brother at the far end of a cable) it must be absolutely real,
devoid of metaphor. Last time out at Wallagundah there'd been
no letter for eight weeks, since well before the Somme. *Pretty
quiet around here, just the occasional raid.* It had had the tone of a
walking tour with rather more than the usual inconveniences.
And yet to Benton now, twelve thousand miles away, the wind
was filled with dying men.

He was praying as he walked and finding it hard. The God
of the orderly universe had withdrawn to its edges, leaving
only this empty wind; it might have been sweeping straight
from France. The inner God, which for so many now was no
more than common integrity, was no more accessible. And
what remained were the iron texts of the New Testament and
the man—if not perhaps God—who'd uttered them. *No servant
can serve two masters ... If my kingdom were of this world ...* There
was nothing of a pulpit draped with Union Jack there, only
injunctions, stony as the slopes they came from. Gospels of the
Impossible. Or the beginnings of courage.

By the fourth circuit's end the wind perhaps had made up its own mind, for a sudden intenser gust seemed to catch him helpless in front of the house and blow him inside, a tall quick figure in a block of light before the door blew shut behind him.

In the bedroom Amy was waiting with Billyjim nuzzled up beside her, the cosmos shrunk to the sphere of a single lamp. 'Woke up again,' she smiled. 'He wouldn't settle. Gone off now though.' Benton studied them for a moment then swept his son off to his room, kissed him once firmly on the ear and came back already undoing his clothes. The fire in the grate was low red coals and in a few more seconds Benton was in bed, his cold face warming against Amy's neck and shoulders, rubbing her with kisses. She laughed and shivered as hands moved over then under pyjamas and nightgown, the husband's straight bones against the wife's allowances of flesh. Together, still laughing softly, they vanished under the blankets.

## 7

The wind had dropped. The front room fire was ashes in the grate. And last night's decision was still there, flat on the table—together with yesterday's *Herald*: MR HUGHES RETURNS: 'VOLUNTARISM HAS FAILED'. Benton scanned again the first couple of inches then looked up towards the door into the hall. His small, blond son, all dressed for the day, was calling him to breakfast. 'All right then, young Billyjim,' and dropping the paper he swept the boy up onto the astonishing heights of his shoulders. 'Let's go!'

'Whee!' shrilled Billyjim as they both ducked under the kitchen door. 'Look out, Mummy, here we come!' Amy turned from the stove and smiled. Despite the highjinks the transition to grace was neatly accomplished; the words for Billyjim a serious game, for Benton and Amy subconscious recommittal. Steam rose from the rolled oats as they passed each other the warmed milk and brown sugar.

'One more day, what do you think?' said Benton in a kind of shorthand. 'Frizelle can hold on that long, especially for that final paragraph.'

'No question of that,' said Amy with a look that to Benton suggested both resistance to signing and the courage to go through with the consequences should he do so. 'No mail till Monday anyway.'

It was the first Saturday in August and, as usual on those five out of six Saturdays that he did not visit Wallagundah, he would spend most of the morning on his sermon. Since May, with some frustration, he had done as the bishop required; there might never have been a war. And even that first sermon, after all, had only been a caution against easy assumptions,

back there in the days before Fromelles and Pozières. 'We feel,'
he'd said, 'in our small way the cause to be just, but to assume
God's view conforms to ours is surely presumptuous, as is the
popular supposition that suffering and dedication will, in itself,
bring spiritual revival.' This, he'd suggested, could only be
prayed for, not taken for granted.

Now, as he sat at his desk in the corner of the drawing room
looking out through the window squares at the churchyard's
bare branches and at the empty road which for three blocks
would become the main street of Geradgery, and heard Amy
speak a little sharply to Billyjim to keep him in the kitchen,
Benton knew the point had been reached. Back in May, as in
that first August, there'd been some kind of role, justifying the
collar's protection. In stress and despair, Benton had argued to
himself, people needed sustenance of the spirit no less than
the care of doctors. The pastoral ministry on the home front
was just as essential as that of the chaplains out in the trenches.
Preaching, visiting, teaching the children, dispensing the
sacraments, bringing the telegrams ... the last he knew now, had
been the beginning—that steady, thin succession, starting a few
days after the landing and falling away only at the year's end. It
set a doubt between the headlines, a doubt which grew as you
walked through the necessary streets to the address, climaxed
as you fumbled for words at the door and left its imprint with
each step back to the vicarage to the unfair safeties of Amy and
Billyjim.

But Gallipoli too had made its inroads—the men sailing
away at the end of eight months, after Lone Pine and the Nek,
leaving nothing but the crosses in Shrapnel Valley, as the papers
called it; hard news all around which even the triumph of two
casualties only at the evacuation did little to soften. 'Pity we
couldn't have done the same thing at the other end,' had been
Amy's only comment, Benton remembered now.

France was different again. There would be no one-day truce
here to bury the dead, no classical echoes of Hector and Achilles,

not if Haig had his way—or Falkenhayn, if you preferred. Now that the lists from Pozières were coming in, Benton began to see it for the shambles it must be, literally, when you translated the thousands of Australians into the hundreds of thousands of Germans, Russians, French and British. The crusade now was becoming a numbness, a day-to-day matter of acceptance and illogical prayers that particular sons and brothers, lovers or husbands, might somehow be spared.

He stared again at the bare outlines of the elms and birches and wrote nothing. At the front, he knew, there must be some similar reduction of hope, but more intense: men clinging fast to a poker hand of memories which the bombardments constantly reduced but could never, short of madness, quite eliminate. Jack's hand could be guessed at: Wallagundah; their mother, Violet; Lyall, maybe. Benton, despite the distances between them, could toy at least with the soiled metaphors for Jack's condition: the pure white terror of the barrage, the endless single moment of the attack, inchoate hatred of the hand to hand. His prayers for Jack persisted doggedly to a God who seemed to back away at their approach. Pointlessly scanning each new list for the B's (there'd have to be a telegram first), Benton was thinking, he knew, more of their mother than of Jack, the impact of the news on that sensitive lean face, those tensely green eyes. She was 'prepared', she'd said once; had been since Gallipoli, but David had only to think of Billyjim's small limbs under the blanket, his head on the pillow, to know the falsity of this.

Half past ten, he saw from his wristwatch, thinking as he did so of Amy who'd given it to him last Christmas, finding it out of fifty pounds her father had sent her as some relief from the austerity of being a clergyman's wife. It was an Omega, very popular these days as a send-off present, and replaced an erratic fob. Benton still felt less than comfortable about it and remembered those mixed but disciplined emotions on the face of her father, a man who'd done well in the Lands Department, when he'd sought his permission to marry his daughter five years back.

Half past ten and no word written. Then, turning now through St Luke for his beginning he saw it, as if for the first time. *And they said, Lord behold, here are two swords. And he said unto them, it is enough.* Though he'd never heard a sermon on it, he could hear himself already declaring it into the oregon beams and rafters of St Jude's, its resonance in the high brick spaces. It had the difficult ambiguity he himself had come to. And there, two verses earlier, *He that hath a purse, let him take it, and likewise his scrip and he that hath no sword, let him sell his garment and buy one.*

'"Here are two swords. And he said unto them, it is enough." I see this,' he would say, 'as one of Christ's most sorrowful and telling insights into man's nature. "Here are two swords," they say, and what is Christ's reply? "It is enough." The tone, I suspect, is the same one He would use today were He to return at the razed village of Pozières.'

As he sat there at his table the entire sermon was stretching out in front of him and, while he normally preferred to speak from notes, he found himself this time writing rapidly in longhand. '"And one of them," says St John later, "smote the servant of the high priest and cut off his right ear. And Jesus answered and said, 'Suffer ye thus far.' And He touched his ear, and healed him."' It was a scene Benton had read and re-read from the age of fourteen but only now, for the first time, did he see it tangible in front of him. 'And note who it is who has his ear cut off. Not just some anonymous member of the lynch mob, as it were, but "the servant of the high priest", the servant of a man and system which Christ in many ways had spent three years overturning. It is not hard to see why Peter attacks him. Some indeed might wonder why he was satisfied with only the ear. Even among the twelve violence was still part of the human condition—and we don't need to be reminded of Christ's dealings with the moneychangers *and* the fact that

Peter, despite his sword, was "the rock on which I shall build my church".' Benton could see through to the end now. One or two further elaborations and then the summing up. It would not be long but it would be genuine.

*Suffer ye thus far. It is enough.* As he paused, then wrote it out again, Benton could almost feel the subtle movement of one phase of his life giving way to another, a moment of sadness and apprehension equally mixed. 'It takes no great leap of the imagination,' he would conclude, 'to link this to our present crisis. Like Peter we have, in wrath and under provocation, attempted to strike down something rigid and unworthy, a system known in the papers as Prussian militarism. Like Peter too we hear Christ's voice, both admonitory and sacrificial, saying beside us: "Suffer ye thus far. It is enough." "And he touched his ear and healed him."' Benton could see himself staring into the helpless silence of the congregation, the slightly tilted ladies' hats, the thinned and greying hair, the scattered children, restless for the sun. He had an impulse of affection, and dismay. 'There are those who say fight on, tear out the Hohenzollern root and branch; there are those who say with Mr Fisher still, fight on to the "Last man and shilling". And there are those like your own vicar, a small number yet perhaps, who cannot in conscience continue their support for the war as they've done these past two years, who feel they must devote what energies and influence they have to an all-out effort for an immediate ceasefire and a negotiated peace, those who, in short, cry out with Christ: "Suffer ye thus far. It is enough."'

As Benton put down the pen he was almost saying it aloud: 'And now in the name of the Father, Son and Holy Ghost, world without end, Amen.' There was a dry constriction in his throat. He walked to the front door and looked out towards the road. It was eleven thirty and the day was just beginning to discover its warmth. He felt on his skin, as much as he saw with his eyes, the winter sun on the gravel street, the stripped trees, the dampness in the gutters. As he looked northwards over the town, woodsmoke bent slightly south towards him. In the slanted overlapping of red and grey roofs, in the faint blue morning haze, in the soiled white gravel of the streets there was that same perfection of imperfect parts he had noticed before— and that inertia, that contentment, which was part of it too.

He went back in, leaving the door open, and began to read his sermon over. It might almost have come from another hand. After three paragraphs there was no point in reading further. It was too exactly what he thought and could not be changed—and neither could the consequences flowing from it. Some could be foreseen (the bishop would make sure of that); others were beyond prediction. He set off down the hall and into the garden where Amy was already turning over a section of soil, ready for the spring. Normally, seeing her at such work, Benton would suffer a mild suffusion of guilt even as he admired her downward thrust with the spade and the way her boot completed the job, pushing in the blade till it levelled with the soil. This time however he hardly noticed the shine on her brow but merely checked how long till lunch; then, murmuring something she didn't catch, seized hold of Billyjim who was scampering around them, swung him up onto his shoulders and strode beside the cool southern flank of the house out onto the street. A few yards on, the boy clamoured to be put down. Benton neatly somersaulted him to the gravel and together they headed off unevenly for the corner.

The air to Benton seemed to hover at a perfect temperature, matched exactly to his face. At the corner they turned left and upwards, climbing, it appeared, for Bald Knob, the squat cone of gums from which only a bit over two months before Benton had watched, mesmerised, the steady advent of Winters' car. To someone looking up the street Billyjim, chattering half-heard beside his father and pulling at his hand, might almost have been mooring Benton to the earth, so springy was his tread already, so lost already to the future.

# PART TWO

## 8

PART TWO

The reaction began, as Benton saw it must, not during the sermon but at the door. Some stared fixedly straight through him and strode on out to the road. One or two were on the point of weeping—Mrs Paget particularly, whose dazed, remaining son Benton remembered from the playground at school. Mrs McGill, however, simply shook his hand as usual and walked on over to her husband Bill waiting at the turnstile. Their son in France undoubtedly kept his own counsel, too. And it was, after all, an immaculate spring morning even though September was still a mouth off, and a few of the more stiffened pensioners edged their way into it, happy enough with that and not too sharp of hearing anyway. Mrs Buchanan, there by chance for the first time in months, swept up directly and shook his hand— as if he had now passed some unseen meridian which in that living room had lain between them. The Bartrims seemed to have taken it the hardest. The father, his son only a week gone, had come up swiftly as if almost to vomit a phrase held down during the final hymn, but then turned suddenly away, not meeting Benton's eye, and paced back to his wife, standing there confused and twisting a glove in her hand. Ignoring others who tried to approach them, they made directly for the turnstile and set off down the road.

The morning was even softer now than it had been an hour before as spring carts, sulkies, a few Fords as well as families on foot had borne in on St Jude's for their weekly reassurance that, notwithstanding the Western Front, there should be no change from Sunday to Sunday—and certainly not in Geradgery. This must at least have been Mrs Giddins' expectation, Benton saw now, as she bounced up to him, elbowing others aside, to say:

'Well, Mr Benton, I must say it's only my respect for your wife that makes me hold my tongue. We don't spend two whole years in patriotic work just to be made fools of. It's a ... disgrace, that's what it is ... a minister of the Church of England. We'll see what the Parish Council has to say on this.' Benton throughout stared vaguely at her nose, the lips a rapid blur beneath it. Suddenly she stopped and before Benton could take in what she'd said or muster a reply, she flounced off round the side of the church, most probably, Benton realised, to 'console' Amy. Helplessly, as others came up to him, he conjured the whole dialogue and smiled to himself just slightly, foreseeing the faultless but annoying way Amy would end the conversation. At another time Benton would have gone off after the woman, but this time he would have to see it out, waiting for the end of that long, dispersing conversation which dwindled away between the trees towards the vehicles and the streets.

As the last few went through the turnstile not quite looking back over their shoulders to where their minister stood alone in his archway, Benton stepped at last inside to help straighten things up—but more, he realised as he did so, to see what Somerton's response would be. Somerton, parish councillor after all, should be an index to the others. In the vestry the choirmaster was just about to leave and seemed upset at not having made it in time.

'I don't know,' said Somerton sideways and upwards over his spectacles, straightening unnecessarily some vestments on a hook. Benton loomed over him in the doorway. 'I just don't know. You could be right, Mr Benton, though I doubt the Council will think so. Nor the bishop, for that matter. You have thought of him, haven't you?'

'Yes, Cyril, I have.'

'Yes, well, if you don't mind, Mr Benton, I'll be off now.' Somerton seemed about to duck under Benton's arm. 'I think you'll find it all in order.' Benton nodded and stepped back.

'You know I did feel ...' But Somerton had already slipped

away, leaving the building to its vicar, the smell of the vanished congregation blending with more permanent ones of cleaning wax, candles, hardwood and dusty brick.

Deferring for the moment any thought of the painful—but manageable—convergence of Mrs Giddins and Amy, Benton walked back into church and sat in the front pew. Even now he was shaking a little. Without kneeling he began at least to think, if not to pray. So much had ended and begun in a single quarter hour. The shedding, it seemed, of one personality and the taking on of another. His life stretched either way, as it must now do also for Amy and Billyjim. For Amy too, he'd known for some time, had been journeying a similar, if more practical, road; and having reached the crucial turn now he'd find her there, he knew already, unflustered and determined. There could be no mere waiting for consequence—that would most surely attend to itself. The shadows, the implications of what he'd just been preaching, lay before him very clearly and there would be others now whose unfamiliar, and less reputable, company he would need to seek out.

## 9

The first week proved choppy, in events and weather too (warm foreshadowings of spring, sleety residues of winter). Amy, Benton noticed, was inclined to leave sentences in the air and took to occasionally hugging him in the hall and kitchen as she'd done in the first year of their marriage, with a similar though different kind of disbelief. She seemed more conscious of his returnings to the house—and the expressions on her face, resolute but wary, came already from the future.

On the Tuesday one small but fiery part arrived. Mrs Giddins, knocking this time formally out front (she more often presumed to call at the back—'just popping in, you know'), presented her letter of resignation from the Women's Guild.

'I'm sorry you feel ...' said Benton, trailing off and staring down vaguely at her sensible brown hat with its who can refuse, in these desperate times, his wholehearted support to the Empire's cause. I've been King and Country all my life and I don't intend turning Irish now.' Amy, hearing it all from the kitchen, smiled. She'd obviously spent some time on that one.

'But surely, Mrs Giddins, it's not a matter ...'

'It is as far as I'm concerned—and there's an end to it.'

'I'm sorry you feel ...' said Benton, trailing off and staring down vaguely at her sensible brown hat with its touch of feather.

'Well, it's done now, isn't it. I can't say I envy your poor wife in all this.' Her concern, Benton saw, was genuine enough, though just a small part of her wider incomprehension. She had that singlemindedness that he himself would soon be needing.

'It's not something we decided overnight, Mrs Giddins,' said Benton, remembering even as he spoke the night itself, those windswept circuits and distant stars.

'No point in talking now, Mr Benton. Here it is.' She thrust the envelope into his hand. 'Take it as you will.'

'But ...' said Benton as he transferred it to the side pocket of his coat.

'Can't stand here talking,' she cut in, looking at him impatiently now, without respect. She might almost have stamped her foot. He'd not seen such a look anywhere in his five years as a vicar. 'Goodbye, Mr Benton.' And Benton, as he recovered, watched her striding down the drive, feeling in that rear view the tone this conversation would take on its way around the town ('King and Country, all my life, I said ... and do you know ...?'). Though he and Amy had often smiled at her excesses, the departure of this woman, and its manner, were a shock even so.

The day before, the Glen Innes Mail had carried away his signature and a one pound postal note to Frizelle in Sydney. The statement would appear, Benton expected, in a fortnight or so. On Wednesday the *Herald*, as a follow-up to Mrs Giddins, declared the Prime Minister's determination to hold a referendum, not just for drill on Saturday afternoons at the local oval but for the Western Front. *Are you in favour of the Government having, in this grave emergency* ...? Given last Sunday and next week's advertisement it would not take the town long to figure where their vicar stood on that one.

Wednesday too brought word from the bishop, a little later than expected. Benton was summoned by Thursday's train to discuss at Bishopscourt *IMPORTANT MATTERS*. Just in reading the telegram Benton could feel the total certainty of the bishop's assumptions, the agility in argument, the condescension, the sheer physical bulk of the man planted behind his mahogany desk. Of all the more certain outcomes of that one quarter hour this might conceivably be the most unpleasant. Whichever way Barker played it, outraged superior or paternal concern, Benton knew he'd failed the test already, even if, in church last Sunday, he'd passed a more important one.

Apart from this the first few days were not so very different; a visit to old Mrs Doughton who 'couldn't get out much now', a walk down to the school to cancel Thursday's class. McPhee, who'd missed last Sunday as usual, had obviously heard all about it and for a man who dealt in certainties seemed most unsure. He failed to look Benton once in the eye and even though it was recess when he arrived there was no offer of tea.

Wednesday evening found out one more gap. Normally on these midweek evenings Somerton and his choir of nine or so were left to practise by themselves, the choirmaster dropping in at the vicarage later to confirm things for Sunday. To Benton, reading after dinner in the drawing room with Amy, the metronomic chords and hesitant descants, so much a part of Somerton's character, were a satisfaction basic to Wednesday nights. They brought back in a weekly tide the chapel at boarding school, the beginnings of his faith. Not to have them filtering across through leadlight and brick was painful— and, he had to suppose, given Somerton's membership of the Council, ominous. The school chapel, he guessed, letting his mind drift as he looked at the steady coals in front of him, would not be much changed—except for the names of the not yet dead and the little crosses for those already spent. Yet another three hundred unquestioning voices, breaking and broken, would be rising to the district's, the Empire's, benevolent God. The feeling for these simplicities, with some elaboration, had led him to St John's where, despite its being merely across the other side of town and just a little further from the world, Benton's faith, and everything else, had slowly become more complex and less tangible until only the more recent and immediate pleasures of Amy and Billyjim could offer a comparable warmth.

It was, Benton had to allow, on this choirless night—and even before last Sunday—a lonely profession. Visiting, preaching, the bringing of sacraments could never quite allay it. Nor did the other three clergy in town; all of them polite enough if met on the street but cut off by centuries' distrust and the different social levels their faiths had found. Not many Anglicans came walking under that railway viaduct to morning service. And only a few Catholics made the journey in reverse. Benton sometimes wondered about that Father Dwyer—if it hadn't been for Amy, what dryness would he himself have come to? There was solitude and there was loneliness. Strange to see them sitting there together in Roget's *Thesaurus*. One to be sought and relished; the other, a pair of socks washed out in a basin in a presbytery or guest house.

So as Benton sat there with his wife, the silence from the church became part of some larger silence which moved out over the half-lit streets, the stations, the backroads, eastwards over the scarp to the Pacific and westwards to the plains, a silence of which Amy at this moment was also a part. He folded the pages of the *Herald* back together and left the headlines staring upwards: *REFERENDUM 28 OCTOBER: 'VOLUNTARISM HAS FAILED', SAYS PRIME MINISTER.* Across from him, Amy, paradoxically, was still at work on one of Mrs Giddins' khaki socks. Amy liked to finish what she started, another thing Benton liked about her. Watching her handle the four quick needles Benton thought of all the socks being knitted in the houses of Geradgery, in New England, in New South Wales, in all the other federated colonies and of all the heels and toes they'd warm, or mean to, in the coming northern winter and how many of those feet might well be blown away before the year was out. The ferocity of some of these knitters (he'd seen them at Mrs Giddins' 'drives' sometimes) amazed him—as if their skill with the needles would somehow help a fellow New Englander over the top to settle the hash of a German. Others, it seemed, untrained for nursing, could find no better way for dealing with the headlines and the dead. And, thought Benton, those other knitters in Saxony, Bavaria, Vienna, Rome, London? Though not any more in the village of Pozières.

Stepping up into his compartment—or dogbox as they'd called them on their trips down to school—Benton slid his briefcase onto the rack and sat with his back to the engine. Nodding once to the compartment's only other occupant, he watched Geradgery slide away: the big successive letters of its name, the platform with its plants in tubs, a few empty sheep-trucks off on a side line, the open backyards with a tinge of green now for the end of winter, the fowlhouses up against fences, the intermittent lines of newly hung washing.

'Going far, reverend?' Benton's concentration was far beyond what he actually saw. The voice, its rasping edge, shook him.

'Just down to Armidale actually,' Benton managed at last, looking for the first time at the man opposite: a broad, impassive, worker's face. 'How about you?'

'Right through. Got a bit of a problem down there as it happens.' Benton, though he felt the man's agitation, attempted to nod away the need for further detail. Given his destination, he was happy enough for the first few minutes anyway just to watch the crippled upland gums and damp pastures slip away and renew themselves, the steady alternation of embankment and cutting. It was the other man who had the need for conversation.

'Yeah, only been down twice before. Sister's had a bit of a shock actually so I thought I'd take my two weeks and well ... see if there was anything I could do. Boss was pretty good about it actually. Couldn't really give much notice.' The stationhand, or that at least was how Benton had placed him, wore self-consciously a pinstriped worsted suit, the pants of which when he stood up would be an inch too short. Benton could somehow tell this even as he rested back in his seat, making the occasional murmurs of polite inattention. 'Yeah, sister's boy, Will, passed away over in France. Got the news a week ago. She's taken it pretty hard, I expect. Only son, he was. No husband either—he shot through way back. Jakes, that was his name, Ted Jakes. Came from round here actually. Took her to Sydney to try his luck in the catering game, or that's what he reckoned. Never worked out though; left her in the end with a ten-year-old kid.'

'What did she do?' said Benton, feeling the unspoken pressure to let the man continue.

'Domestic service. You know, hotels, that sort of thing. Will had to leave school, of course. Bright lad too. Used to reckon I was his favourite uncle. Lived in one of them terrace houses in Glebe. You know Glebe?' Benton nodded vaguely, seeing the blood-fused face of Barker a good deal more closely than the one opposite. 'Could've done a lot with himself, young Will, if he'd had the chance.'

Benton felt the train tilt downwards, down the long cutting and through the scrappy hillside trees you could see from the top of Bald Knob. He was uneasily conscious yet again of the way a clerical collar reduced men to either silence or confession. The man brought back uncomfortably the helpnessness Benton felt when visiting east of the viaduct; he was a milder, better-disposed version of the same distances and failures. So now after confession it was silence again. Not until the last mile or so along the valley into Armidale between orchards and farms did either of them speak.

'Well, looks like they'll all be going now, eh?' The stationhand was looking out over a few acres of apple trees in flower. 'What do you reckon, reverend?' Benton stared at him blankly, aware more of the inept term of address than of what he was trying to say. 'This referendum. Pretty sure to get through, if you ask me.' For a long moment Benton still said nothing. The apple orchard slipped away to the right.

'I wouldn't be too sure of that,' said Benton at last. 'People are starting to realise ...' Benton, as he registered the pure incomprehension on the stationhand's face, could see its variant on Barker's. 'If half the energies put into recruiting were spent on finding a way to peace it could all be over in a matter of months. We could have the troops home.'

'You mean ... I thought all you people ...'

'Well,' said Benton, with the same reckless relief he had felt last Sunday, 'now you know one who's not. And there'll be more, you can be pretty sure of that.' There was, he knew, an anger, even a self-righteousness in his tone that had no place there. In a way he was practising on this man for his moment with Barker and he felt vaguely ashamed.

'But only last week I saw the bishop himself up at Glen Innes, outside the post office there. Pretty fiery he was, too. You know, slackers, shirkers, all that sort of thing.'

Benton looked directly into the man's eyes. 'Now you know why I'm getting off at Armidale then.'

The expression on the man's weathered face seemed to simplify as Benton watched it. 'Yeah, well,' he said, 'I never could see the point of Will going anyway, to tell the truth.'

The train was banging finally to a halt. Benton reached upwards, swaying, for his briefcase. There was a sepia view of Sydney Harbour under glass in front of him. 'Hope things aren't too bad when you get there.' And for a moment Benton saw the sister at her Glebe front door and knew the expression exactly.

'Yeah, thanks anyway,' said the stationhand, ready now, Benton could see, to sink back into himself for the rest of the journey. The story, it seemed, would be told once only and Benton, as he swung open the door and stepped down, regretted not having paid it closer attention. He looked back and nodded to the face in the window, a granite slab—which suddenly split with the first smile of thirty miles. The window went up abruptly. 'Best of luck with the big feller, anyway.'

At ten exactly the sulky from the railway pulled up at Bishopscourt behind St Peter's. It was still a light, clear morning. Miss Pym, the bishop's secretary, having sat Benton down for the mandatory ten-minute wait (meditation? contrition?) pointedly ignored him. Then Bishop Barker swung back the door and conducted him goodnaturedly enough into the walnut-panelled, leather-volumed room which had so concentrated Benton's thoughts on the thirty miles downhill from Geradgery. Barker indicated the usual low armchair. There was a suitable pause. Benton remembered, irrelevantly, perhaps from the gesture that had seated him, something indefinite about Sandhurst, some synod gossip ... a false start in the Guards? Or was that a brother?

'Well, Benton, my son,' Barker began, 'it seems I haven't made myself sufficiently clear.' Benton saw now the way it would be played, but Barker suddenly went on with growing impatience. 'Shall I perhaps run over it again? The people, yes, David, the parish, the diocese, are looking to us for a lead. They don't want doubts and half-baked second thoughts; they don't want the cosy fireside ruminations of someone who, let us face it, doesn't have to go anyway.' Barker winced slightly as he said it, as if he'd surprised even himself with his poor taste or touched some nerve of his own he'd not known was there. It was just enough to give Benton courage.

'They're not, my Lord, what you call cosy ruminations. It's just that ... well ... after two whole years of rounding them up and cheering them off, I ... and, I suppose, the telegrams.' Adding the last, he realised that Barker almost certainly would have delegated this task to his deacon or even to Denning-Jones, the dean. '... And the lists, Gallipoli, Pozières, Sir Ian Hamilton, Sir Douglas Haig.' He spelled them out rhythmically, as if the first of a long succession, a cynical edge to the 'sirs' he'd not quite intended.

The bishop leaned back in his chair, the broad desk between them. The barrel chest and ample stomach formed, as Benton had noticed before, a single hemisphere. Looking at that purple stock, Benton thought irreverently and in a flash of the flesh underneath, the singlet, white folds of skin perhaps, saw the image of that bulk on top of the shadowy, overbred wife he'd seen at synod suppers, and wondered again why they'd not had children.

'Now, look here, Benton. You do know the stand the whole church has taken on this. It's not just the Parish Council, you know. You've seen the synod resolutions. You'll be a lonely man if you persist with this, you may be sure of that.' Barker looked suddenly out the window at what Benton saw too was a greening elm. 'That's if you wish to stay on at all.' The bishop looked back once to see his thrust take effect and then went on. 'But that, I suppose, is something we needn't look into at this point, assuming, even after last Sunday, you're prepared to desist. Perhaps silence is the best we can expect now.' He gave a humourless laugh and looked back over his shoulder. 'Not much likelihood of Captain Winters inviting *you* back to the colours, I should think.' Benton said nothing, running his eye along the shelves. 'Well, I do have your assurance on that, do I not? That we may expect no more of these ... treasonable maunderings.' As the bishop relished his own felicity of phrase Benton rose abruptly from his chair and made for the door.

'I'm afraid, bishop, I can give you no such assurance.' His hand was on the knob now and he spoke back over his shoulder: 'I must preach according to my conscience. Anything less would be unthinkable.' Even before he'd finished, the bishop, with a breakaway's burst of speed, shot around his desk and seized his vicar by the lapels, shaking him and shouting upwards into his face.

'And what, confound it, does pro-German defeatism have to do with Christ's teaching? We are fighting here for the values of British and Christian civilisation. You don't imagine you'd be entitled to the luxury of your opinion in Prussia, do you? They make very short work of your sort there, I can tell you.' Benton, despite the man's strength, somehow managed to free himself.

'I see no point, bishop, in discussing this in the present circumstances. This whole business is profoundly regrettable but I have no other choice.' Though he had at least the satisfaction of his own sincerity, Benton heard also in another part of his mind the unwelcome echo of little Miss Rosemary Steggart, that primness. 'I shall not only speak against conscription but also against the war—from the pulpit and elsewhere.'

Miss Pym, Benton saw as he plunged out, had never been so shocked. Out in the air again he strode past the cathedral, large but humanly proportioned, on his right. Some time later that day, he knew, he would be back to meditate in its roomy silences but now, as if Barker were physically in pursuit (anything was possible, he felt), he strode away downhill towards the main street. Even in such a crisis there were still a couple of things to be got for Amy, and having nothing to do till the five o'clock train north, he thought he might allow himself a secular hour or so in the City Café with the latest *Bulletin*. That at least would get his heart rate down. It was still just half past ten and, not yet being Friday, the main street with its kerb-to-kerb asphalt was almost empty. Working his way along beneath the verandas, Benton managed to get the two particular shades of cotton at the haberdasher's for Amy, mused a while at the newsagent's and stationer's, glanced sidelong into the dark interiors of three successive hotels and, keeping half an eye out for the Universal Service League conscription posters which he knew must soon be going up, came at length to the City Café. There, having set himself up at a table and bench and begun a thin milk coffee, he opened his *Bulletin*. The waitress clattered away back into the kitchen.

In many ways Barker's summons had been just what he needed—a day away from the illusory continuities of Geradgery to consider his next move—and, maybe, the move beyond that. The future was a landscape without either distance or middle ground. Amy, he knew, saw further into it but they had not yet discussed how far. Idly he flipped the pages as if the whole fiasco with his bishop might somehow slip away between them. Patent medicines, automobile advertisements, cartoons ... A languid young socialite with scarf chatting to a soldier whose mate discreetly stared into a merchant's window. *She: Your friend is just too sweet for words. He: Well, maybe. He settled ten Huns before breakfast one morning.*

Doggerel, too, scattered throughout.

> *Is it football still or the picture show,*
> *The pub, and the betting odds,*
> *When your brothers stand to the tyrant's blow*
> *And England's cause is God's?*

A parody of Bishop Barker, M.A., D.D.? Or a summary of that two years' clerical handwringing over the unrepentant whose metamorphosis via sacrifice had been so universally predicted? Benton stared unseeingly out into the deserted main street. Moral renewal, national purpose, an end to the demon drink and even, for some of his Methodist colleagues, dancing. Something of that first war Sunday returned for a moment: the brassy phrases, a young man or two already in khaki and the handshakes at the church front door binding a preacher to what he'd said. He looked at the pale remains of his coffee and skimmed the patriotic gossip of 'A Woman's Letter'. With Barker's 'treasonable maunderings' still sounding in his ears and in the face of all his thought so far, Benton could still wonder whether, in 1916, drinking coffee and reading magazines in a country town on Thursday morning at the far end of the world was quite the right place for a fit twenty-nine year old to be.

Certainly some, he reminded himself later in the cathedral, had gone; the gallant chaplains of the anecdotes who took their faith to the trenches but never quite over the top. Though Benton himself in the years of his enthusiasm had never considered it (Amy and Billyjim being his two best reasons), the one-year tour was always oversubscribed. Men he'd known at St John's (that man Watkins for one) had begged their bishops to let them go. Where else could a genuine Christian be more required than on the battlefield? The wrecked cathedrals, the tilted shrines had their particular poignance. One or two chaplains were rumoured, in a bloody moment, to have seized a .303 and gone in with the rest; a logical step when you thought about it—to do otherwise would be like going to bed with a naked woman and not succumbing. An image of Amy under the covers disconcerted him. *Where do you stand when a German's intent on despoiling your daughter, violating your wife, murdering your mother?* It was almost a liturgy. He'd read it again last week. *The raping of nuns.* Such visions, threadbare though they were, never quite wore out their power—you saw the skirts go over the heads. But, as Amy had sardonically suggested not so long ago, was that the Kaiser's main war aim? And would he sail twelve thousand miles to do it; and would the French, thought Benton, sweeping into Köln be any different from the Germans in Liège? The despoilers meanwhile were piling up impartially at Verdun and the Somme.

Sitting (and, once, kneeling) in the back pew, Benton watched the dust motes in the stained shafts of afternoon light and felt them continue through the darker spaces up to the nave where a high brass lamp was burning. Earlier he'd tried to pray but the God he'd known, or wished to know, had shrunk, as if on second thoughts, back from the Gospels to the prophets—a national god now with a sharp sense of injury and a taste for vengeance. Christ himself, remained—not much diminished— but more as a figure to wonder at than a god to pray to; Christ the man, a moral template defying copy but setting the measure even so for how far one fell short; an absolute in courage and, in his softer moments, wisdom. *Let him who is without sin ...* Each man finds the Christ he needs, Benton knew now. Barker's, no doubt, next-door in Bishopscourt, was muscular and medieval, a vizored seeker of Holy Grails, with gallantry and decency in equal proportion.

After ninety minutes more Benton had not really prayed at all but nevertheless had got what he'd come for—or enough of it to go on with. Walking back the dozen or so blocks to the station and noting the flattened light against the dark brown sides of houses he took, through the cathedral city's grid, the zigzag closest to diagonal. And so, before the Mail steamed in, had half an hour to wait, his briefcase (except for Amy's two reels of cotton) empty on his knees.

## II

The following Sunday as he came in from the vestry Benton saw at a glance his numbers down to half—women, mainly, and older men. There was a forlorn but also a more intimate, perhaps defensive air, among them. Some, he knew, with a lifetime of Sunday mornings behind them, were not about to leave now; a few, he hoped, were there relieved at having had their own two years' unease given voice. Some, maybe, were curious to see what further recklessness might follow.

'Dearly beloved brethren, the Scripture moveth us in sundry places ...' The choir was down to four, and unconducted (Somerton, clearly, had made up his mind), but in the opening hymn it seemed determined to fill out the spaces. In the sermon at the end Benton, despite his altitude, spoke almost as if he himself were down in the pews. Leaving the war aside, though not this time at Barker's bidding, he began with the humanity of Christ, the agony of the crucifixion, the nails, the spear, the sop with vinegar. 'Nothing we believe about the resurrection,' he said, 'diminishes the humanity of that death and what it represented. It was a death designed, it seems to me, to drive us back continually upon his message, to have us accept its absolutes as fully as we can.' And as he spoke Benton could feel the pressure of what he'd said bending the outlines of his own life. 'It is not a faith, this human death tells us, to be watered down or turned to worldly or transient purposes. It is a faith which in the end survives the centuries of self-seeking and distortion imposed upon it.' Benton, though he had his notes, hardly referred to them at all. The words were discovering a direction of their own and this, in a way, forced him to finish abruptly, wary at last of where they might take him.

As the last hymn rang thinly in the rafters Benton made his way directly to the front door and stood for a moment gulping the spring air. The sermons for the weeks ahead seemed already to be written, each one more basic, more minimal, than the last, wearing away each week towards a core, the smallness and toughness of which he could now only guess at. *I believe in God, the Father Almighty, Maker of Heaven and earth.* That might well be the first to go. More obvious at night, he knew, that meaninglessness between the stars ... and yet now, by the front door and looking through the greening English trees, how could a faith slip away like that? The calloused firmness of these handshakes, the gloved hands of shopkeepers' wives, the toughened claws of stooped old ladies clutching unrepentant to their lives ... There had to be connections somewhere.

12

In a town like Geradgery, Benton had long thought, the future arrived so slowly it was all you could do to notice it. Now, however, in this last week and a half, it had swept in like a sharp spring change. The next gust blew on Tuesday, about four thirty, as Billyjim came rattling down the hall to Benton and Amy in the kitchen. 'Daddy, Daddy, there's someone ...' And now Benton heard it too, the second knock, light but definite.

'Afternoon, reverend,' said the stranger, lifting off a blue peaked cap. 'You won't know me, I guess.' His smile, in a face once tanned and now faded, had just the edge of a smirk. Benton finally placed the uniform, worn with slightly defiant slackness. 'Spenser's the name, Bert Spenser. Seen you at the station; though I doubt if you saw me. Last Thursday, I think it was.' He was a short, wiry man who looked up at Benton with neither deference nor goodwill.

'Ah, yes,' said Benton. 'Come in. No point in talking out here.' Stooping over Spenser, almost solicitously, he conducted him into the drawing room. The railwayman sat on the sofa under the window as Winters had done five months before. Benton was forced to think briefly of that similarly capped but otherwise totally different figure, perched and pacing about the room. Like Winters, Spenser too got straight to the point.

'We heard what they reckon you're saying in church these days. Thought you might be able to help us out a bit.' Us? thought Benton as Spenser paused and looked more carefully around the room, taking in the space, the bookshelves, Amy's eight-day clock on the mantel. 'A motion against conscription went through a meeting of ours down at Central on the weekend. The local branch are putting on a meeting at the Institute this

Friday night.' Benton could picture the little hall just near the station, a kind of fruit box on stilts. Spenser looked him squarely in the eye. 'They reckoned you might like to speak. How about it? From what I hear ...'

'Not quite the same thing though,' said Benton, giving himself a chance to fathom the man's expression. He remembered something like it at the back door of Wallagundah homestead when he was ten—a stockman ill-temperedly giving notice. Had Spenser spoken against the proposal but been sent along to make it anyway? Where was the Rev. Benton in the strike of '91? Or in August, '14, for that matter?

'If what we hear going round is right, you're not only against conscription but the whole box and dice. A real Boche lover, if some of the cockies can be believed. Can't see where the problem is.'

'Who else have you got?'

'Well,' said Spenser, relaxing a little into the sofa, 'there's me. And that ex-digger fellow. What's his name now? Wally Tippet, yes. Turns out he's not too happy with his pension. Lost a leg at the Dardanelles apparently.' Benton said nothing, wondering now what troubles Spenser might have had with the recruiters himself. The wrinkles, and the half-scowl into which they'd collected, made him forty-five at least but there'd be times he could be taken for less. No doubt the captain would have found a way if Spenser had wanted to put his age down.

'It's only the beginning out here, you know,' Spenser went on. 'It's not only us unionists who'll be fighting it. There'll be cockies and the big graziers too, you wait and see. Who's going to do the work while Johnny's in the army, eh? That's the way they're thinking now. King, Country and Capital. That's the one that really counts.'

Spenser seemed rather proud of his analysis. He had the look, Benton saw, of a man for whom a little learning must only confirm what he knows already. Benton's decision, a fortnight old, though clear at the time was already growing cloudy in its

consequences. His whole sensibility wished Spenser out the
door (he was so much the type that Benton all his life had failed
with or managed to sidestep—the hapless families across there
under the viaduct, the stockmen out at Wallagundah). But
the wished-for departure did not occur till Benton's own logic
had won his agreement to speak. Certainly, thought Benton as
Spenser picked up his cap and headed for the door, they were
comrades in the same campaign but, as the man set off down
the road towards town, his walk, Benton observed, had more
than a measure of triumph about it.

## 13

'Yes,' said Bert Spenser, winding it up now, 'like most of you I've got a good few mates who rushed in to join up—and a good few who've paid the price. Might almost've volunteered myself if I'd been a bit younger.' He looked out into the packed, ill-lit audience of forty or so, a trestle table draped with a calico *VOTE NO* in front of him.

'Sixteen thousand blokes a month, I say it again. That's what Billy wants, you know. That's what Haig and the duchess of whatshisname told him. As if we hadn't already given 'em more than they deserve ... and had them wasted.'

'It's a trade war, Bert, and you know it,' came a voice near the front.

'Yes, Sam,' Spenser agreed, 'whatever it was in the beginning it's a trade war now. We don't need the good archbishop down in Melbourne to tell us that.' There was a localised burst of applause. 'Which reminds me, speaking of the church, the Church of England in this case, we just happen to have our very own representative here tonight.' He paused and smiled with an edge of condescension at Benton down the far end of the table. 'The Reverend David Benton, who's seen the light at last, you might say.'

Spenser at one stage had looked to be set for a long innings, the arguments coming to him like cards from the air. Now suddenly Benton, smarting from Spenser's little snideness, was on his feet. Clasping a small square of paper he stared mutely into the forty, close-packed faces. He felt acutely the need of a pulpit, its battlemented cover for notes, and an admiring front row of ladies to ease him into voice.

'Ladies and gentlemen, members of the union,' he began,

forgetting its exact name and regretting immediately the
distinction implied. Unionists or gentlemen? There was that
streak of elocution too, as foreign to these wooden walls as the
blurred faces out there were to him. 'I speak tonight not so much
as a clergyman but as a citizen; a man who once supported
this war and all that the Allies seemed to stand for, but a man
who now, with some reluctance but inevitably nevertheless,
confesses his mistake.'

'Nice to hear it anyway,' said a not unfriendly voice up the
back somewhere.

'Could've been a bit more use earlier on though,' came a less
friendly one.

'Yes,' said Benton. 'I can understand such comments and
that, in a way, is why I stand here tonight. I cannot now see,
and believe me I've looked very hard, how anyone can square
a decision to fight on to unconditional surrender with a single
word of the New Testament. How, I ask, can we in the spirit of
Christ, continue this war a moment further without making
some drastic and all-out effort to end it?' He stopped and let the
question hang and saw that for some down there in the front
row he might just as well have been speaking classical Greek.
They seemed to be waiting for a translation.

'Easy enough for you, reverend,' said someone laconically
over near the door. 'You're not under any pressure. Priests and
politicians, the only two exceptions if Billy has his way. Funny
that.'

There'd been a time not so long back when such a truth
might well have crushed him, but now, even with this shadowy
and elusive audience, he felt able to say: 'Don't think, my
friend, I haven't been aware of that every day of this conflict.
My only wish is that every man among you, every man across
Australia, should be similarly excepted. Mr Hughes is asking us
for sixteen thousand five hundred men a month to prolong the
agony indefinitely. I ask you to do everything in your power to
cut it short—and that, ladies and gentlemen, means voting NO

on 28 October. Thank you, Mr Spenser, for asking me to speak.'
Benton nodded slightly into the small applause (not seeing
any ladies) and sat down as Spenser rose with an impresario's
flourish to introduce his main attraction.

'And, now, ladies and gentlemen, for the most important
speaker of the evening, ex-Lance Corporal Wally Tippet,
unsung hero of the Dardanelles, a man who's given a limb
for his country and, like the worker he is, has suffered pretty
shabby treatment since. We're proud to have you, Wally.' Tippet
dragged a crutch under his right armpit and stood up behind
the table, wavering a moment or two before beginning. At
the table's end Benton had long since caught a sour whiff of
alcohol. Spenser had taken a risk and saved his soldier till last.
There was something very unnerving about Tippet. Physically
he was still young, twenty-two perhaps, but under the patina
of his experience, Benton could see, was a more permanent
immaturity which would never quite come to terms with his
mutilation.

'Well, ladies and gentlemen, as you can see,' Tippet began,
knocking his crutch against the table, 'I've been to Gallipoli—
which is more than most of you have, I reckon. Yes, I was in
the landing with the boys of the First Division, the heroes of
the Dardanelles, what's left of 'em.' The man's drunkenness
seemed to validate rather than undermine his words. Benton's
was not the only face with a complicated wince. 'Well, I did my
bit, as they say—and Jacko got his bit—as they don't say. And a
nice Red Cross girlie met me off the boat, very sympathetic she
was—for at least a week till the next lot of blokes came in. And
now I'm back with me old mum in Armidale on seven and six
a week. And most of you on three pound ten at least. The local
War Service boys have kicked in another fifteen bob just to put
it up over the guinea.' He wavered blankly for a moment until
another point suggested itself. 'Don't get me wrong. I haven't
got anything against the boys of the A.I.F., sterling blokes to a
man. Don't know what they think of the Empire now, but they

surely do look after their mates—which is more than I can say
for Billy Hughes and his Defence Minister, George Pearce. Six
bob a day they give you to go and seven and six a week when you
get back minus a leg. You figure that.' Tippet stared down into
the forty faces. The wits up the back were notably silent. "'Last
man and last shilling", they used to say. Well, I'll believe the
first bit but they're still a fair way off the second if you ask me.'
Casting one short inquiring look at Spenser, Tippet suddenly
collapsed into his chair and, laughing without humour, called:
'Vote NO, that's the ticket!'

There was a loud, sustained response. Benton himself was
still clapping as Spenser got up to close the meeting. Within
five minutes the room was empty. Neither Spenser nor Benton
had any wish, it seemed, to stay on talking. Spenser would have
enough trouble just getting Tippet back to the Hibernian.

Benton, walking back to Amy under a sky of broken cloud,
felt even more uncomfortable than he had while speaking or in
leaving, a few rough slaps of sympathy to send him on his way.
Thinking of Barker, and then by extension of all his secular
equivalents, he could hear the jibes in saloon bars all across
New England—slackers, shirkers, cowards. How did that bit of
doggerel go?

*Is it the German blood in your veins,*
  *Or is it the yellow streak?*
*Maybe you're deaf and dumb and blind,*
  *Or is it your 'art that's weak?*

St Jude's, as Benton approached it now, was silhouetted
against cloud, its peaked roof and cross defined against white.
Of the vicarage next-door he could see almost nothing. Normally there'd be a lamp in the front room. Now a slit of light down
the side from the kitchen was all he could see. And that was
where he found them: Amy still nursing a sobbing Billyjim and
almost in tears herself. Not yet knowing why and never having

felt anything like it since school (even in the confrontation with
Barker), Benton was shaken with anger. He took both of them
in his arms. 'Some boys,' Amy managed at last, 'threw rocks on
the roof, big ones, might have broken the slates. Woke him up
with their foolishness.'

Benton stepped back from the embrace, taking Billyjim
with him. 'Couldn't quite catch what they were calling,' Amy
went on. '"Hun lover", it might have been. About quarter of an
hour ago.' Though it was obviously too late, Benton, rocking
his son now in his arms, shuffled through the chances anyway.
Twelve year olds from the school? Cockies' sons on their way
home from the Royal, putting each other up to it and hot for
their eighteenth birthday? There'd been, he knew, a Win the
War rally that afternoon outside the post office just as the
shops closed—an amateur one, no doubt, without the Captain's
expertise. Recalling that pink, taut man on the edge of the sofa,
Benton knew instinctively that by now Winters had been told
everything. For a moment, even as he held his child in his arms
asleep, Benton felt that distant, unseen scorn, like a schoolboy
surprised in some small, unworthy act, a petty theft perhaps in
the change rooms.

'And we thought the decision would be the hard part,' said
Amy, half-smiling now. As they took Billyjim together to his
room Benton couldn't shake Winters from his mind. The captain
too, he saw, would have his own humiliations: the endless small
town Schools of Art with one recruit only (what happened,
Benton wondered, to that pale-faced boy at the rally back in
May?); the sardonic interjections; the counting out and straight
abuse in the bigger towns; the abasement awaiting anyone who,
like Christ, goes into the market place with a single idea and
looks for converts. Objector or recruiter, the spectrum that held
them was almost a circle, uniting them, despite themselves, in
opposite extremes—broken separately on the same wheel.

'And to have to make it for your children,' Amy went on, as
they stood there looking down together at Billyjim's head on

the pillow, 'that's what really hurts.' She leaned up hard against David's chest and as he put his arms around her he didn't try prayer or mention God's purpose. The resources would have to be within them. Looking past Amy's shoulder at the clarity of Billyjim's face caught in a line of lamplight from the kitchen, Benton for the moment believed it might be so.

## 14

Working over his New Testament next morning and looking up from his desk at the elms with their clear unfurling leaves, Benton found again as he'd done in the cathedral that foreground Christ and background God, that vengeful patriarch so useful to Barker and his friends—*an eye for an eye*. From all the thousands of oaken pulpits across the country you could almost sniff the goat hair burning, like the branding iron's whiff on a calf's rump. He remembered this morning as he hadn't done for years that demiurge of Marcion from his Church History at St John's—the inferior Old Testament creator-judge, outclassed by the true New Testament God revealed by Jesus. Heresy, of course, as was that skew-whiff trinity of Arius, his Christ who at one time had not existed—and was all the more human for that. Heresies, like peace, were never quite abandoned; they tended to recur as needed.

After lunch, with little written, Benton took his son on a long, slow walk through the western, 'better', side of town, lifting him sometimes on his shoulders (unseemly he knew for a minister on a public street but that didn't stop him as once it had), waiting sometimes as Billyjim chattered off after sticks or bits of glass in gutters or fearlessly bailed up yelping terriers behind their paling fences. The scattered cloud of last night had drifted east, leaving a soft mid-afternoon. The stony rain of last night had vanished also, it seemed, for Billyjim—along with whatever dreams had left him as he woke and slipped across the hall into his parents' bed. Though Benton's strange, unwelcome anger had gone now, its residue persisted somewhere, taking the edge off the weather.

The second Sunday (as Benton thought of it, measuring everything now from that crucial sermon) was overcast with low running cloud. Its service was a scaled-down version of the first and again he did not directly speak of the war, deciding that the congregation's very presence must be at least a toleration of his views if not support. What could he add and who could be unaware of his railway speech on Friday? Their burden was sufficient after all. At the front door afterwards young Tom Dalloway came up to let him know that the tennis club had had to withdraw from the competition through lack of players. Considering how he quietly enjoyed his occasional, unobtrusive appearances on Saturday afternoons to cheer the youngsters on and how, much earlier back at St John's his angular body (along with Frizelle's more serious one) had dashed good-humouredly about the court, Benton was surprised at how little he regretted it. It was just another small part of the pattern. Timber, bricks and slate were as solid as ever but the church itself was slipping away; the subtle linkages were failing. He thought of the irrepressible Mrs Giddins sitting stonily at home (or harrying the Parish Council), of Cyril Somerton digging uneasily in his garden.

More crucial, perhaps, was the way Bishop Barker had not yet spelt out the obvious. After that lapel-grabbing dash across the study nothing could be unexpected. He had merely, Benton knew, with a little formal assistance from the Parish Council, to sign a simple declaration to have Benton's licence to officiate withdrawn, making him in fact what he almost was already, vicar without church, breadwinner without bread. Even so on that grey windy morning as he stood there and watched the last of his diminished congregation file out through the turnstile, he did not toy with recantation. It had a leisurely, late-night attraction (as no doubt it had had for Marcion and Arius), but as a daylight possibility it did not exist.

At ten that night, with the cloud even lower, Benton looked out through the drawing room windows and saw through its tight squares his own figure reflected on the dark. It was as if man and image had suddenly swapped places and Benton himself was out there peering in, some destitute or tramp watching a country vicar at ease by his mantelpiece, his wife knitting and caught at the point of speech. Not able to bring himself to knock, the tramp he might have been turned aside and staggered away downhill into the wind.

*14 Langlee Ave,*
*Waverley*
*7.9.16*

*Dear David,*

   *No doubt by the time you get this you will have seen our statement in Saturday's Herald. Events may have overtaken us somewhat but only to make our position more imperative. There has been nothing in my life so far more important than this course we are currently set upon. Certainly it will bring us no popularity but when did the true follower of Christ fear that?*

   *A number of my colleagues in the Anti-Conscription League (and in the Peace Society) are planning a big rally for the Saturday before the referendum. They, and I, feel that a speech from an Anglican minister such as yourself would be of great value to the cause. Do let me know as soon as you can. It will be in the Domain on the Saturday afternoon (we're not allowed to hire a hall, of course).*

*Yours,*
*Jeremy*

*P.S. Do you remember Philip Watkins? I had a letter from him the other day (first in six years) and remembering how you always liked to hear both sides I've put it in. He went over as a chaplain earlier in the year.*

   Frizelle had also included a couple of posters. Benton hauled them out of the packet and spread them on his desk. *Ten Reasons for Voting No.* The crudity of both typeface and argument forced him to remind himself of his commitment to the same objective. There was something of the same unease or embarrassment that he felt in his dealings with Spenser. Watkins' letter itself was written in a clear, black, leisurely hand, certainly not under bombardment.

*I've been thinking quite a bit lately,* the letter confessed, *about that little class of ours. Some of the faces are clear enough, others, I find, have gone completely. Your mother's address, for some strange reason, is the only one I now recall (that strange way of spelling Langlee?). I wonder if you still remember that debating speech of yours against the death penalty. 'Nothing can justify the taking of a human life.' That, I think, was your general drift. Well I may say the months I've seen over here have given me some thought on that score.*

*From what I remember I don't imagine you've been applying for a tour as chaplain. It's not an easy role. One is always slightly apart, an honorary officer, without real training; ducking the same shells, of course, but never quite going over the top. Most of the men prefer it this way, I think. It ties them back to something they never really lose, the half-forgotten decencies of home. Not that they aren't tough. Everything here boils down to the sheer fact of killing Germans. Sometimes among the wounded at an aid post or back from the line there's a slight softening. They take what they need, what they can, of our ritual. The burials, particularly, are important, though not always possible. A few carry the faith they brought with them, somewhat tempered of course, though they wear it lightly enough and rarely speak of it even to us. This feeling for their mates bends their theology a little. There are quite a few unabsolved Catholics, for instance, whom their friends expect to see in Heaven. Not a few agnostics, too, if it comes to that. And in the midst of all this it's a reckless man indeed who would presume to know God's way precisely.*

*Ask them why they fight, if you were thoughtless enough, and they'd give you no ideal, other than the vague conviction that it has to be done or that the world must somehow be a better place afterwards. King, Country and, I fear, God for most are mere abstractions—as is Prussian militarism. They fight, it seems to me, for their comrades, the living and the dead, the latter, even if blown apart beside them, are somehow no more distant than a transfer to another unit. Some,*

*we know, joined up for the money, others on a spree, many under*
*that silent pressure which by the time they got here was already*
*irrelevant. You hear no reference to it now.*

*Given what I remember from St John's I guess you have no*
*great enthusiasm for this war and that, I suppose, is partly why I*
*write. The war undoubtedly began in opposition to God's will and*
*in rejection of His offered redemption but now, over here, I think I*
*see a little good come out of it. The men, though brutal enough in an*
*attack, care more for each other here than they ever would have at*
*home. Those who get back will be haunted, no doubt, but they'll have*
*something irreplaceable as well. The need for man's redemption and*
*his potential for it seem clearer to me over here than they ever did in*
*Armidale or Sydney. God, I suspect, might be on our side after all—if*
*not for a simple victory over Germany then for something we don't*
*quite yet see beyond that.*

*Maybe I can track you down early next year when my stint is*
*finished and we can talk this over peacefully somewhere.*

*Yours in Christ,*
*Philip Watkins*

Benton folded the letters and posters back in the packet.
No doubt to Frizelle, Watkins would be impressionable and
woolly-minded but to Benton, taken up as he was with his
new opinions, Watkins' measured, tentative certainties were in
their way more persuasive than either of the opposed simplicities espoused by Frizelle or Barker. If Watkins had not been a
very memorable classmate (and Benton did in fact have trouble picturing his face), you had at least to concede his physical
courage. But of course there were still the chaplains on the other side, sustaining their men, or trying to, in the official con-
victions, helping them through another year of suffering and
killing—two school football teams almost, with chaplains as
coaches barracking from the sidelines in a game gone endlessly
beyond the final whistle. Yes, the chaplains didn't do the killing

but they helped. Why would they be tolerated if they didn't? As Frizelle said, it was time to take a clearer view, to actually do something and not simply consent to be turned on the wheels of the juggernaut. But Benton, even so, did not immediately send his agreement to speak. Amy too, dark-haired and smiling, declaring morning tea there in the doorway, would have to have her say. As would the bishop, one way or another.

'There's not too much doubt what it means then,' Amy was saying a little later, the teapot between them on the kitchen table. 'You speak down there and he'll feel there are no options left him—that's if he's inclined to options anyway.'

'When you think of last Thursday,' said David, 'the way he jumped across that study, it's a wonder he hasn't made his move already.' He thought suddenly of poor Cyril Somerton—and the way Mrs Giddins would have bailed him up over the counter. 'He'd have no trouble with the Council.'

'You're still his only snake in the woodpile though—he could be still hoping you'll come round.' She poured out two cups.

'Not after last Thursday, I think.'

'And if he does withdraw it?' Amy looked straight at him with that frankness of forehead which had so taken him at a church hall supper down in Sydney six years back—and still did. 'Not that the stipend is so very grand anyway,' she added with a smile in just the corner of her mouth.

'Could work for Lyall, I guess. He's been shorthanded, I know—though I'm not too sure what he'd think in the circumstances.' Benton paused and looked down at the table. 'Haven't quite told mother yet, either.'

'What about in an office somewhere, down in Sydney? You're got your matriculation, after all, even if the diploma's ...' She tailed off, appearing to see its pointlessness. Sydney at least would be close to her father but that, Benton knew, was only a small consideration. He was moved and faintly ashamed at her dedication. More than he deserved, as Mrs Giddins would say.

'I'm not sure what I'd do,' said Benton, reaching a hand out
to her across the tea cups, 'if I didn't have you along.'

'Watch out for the tea,' said Amy, pushing the pot to one side.
He smiled and pulled back his hand. Her face was impatience
and affection equally joined. He went on anyway.

'Especially when I think of Billyjim. It won't do him any
good.' He looked at her again directly. 'Though I suppose it's
a little easier to live with someone if he can already live with
himself.' And now Benton, as he saw the words register on Amy's
face, knew his decision already made. A long shiver seemed to
run up his back from the kitchen chair as he saw himself in a
single vivid image perched on a wagonette, pitching his voice
to the crowded thousands and away out over their heads to
the elephantine Moreton Bays and beyond them again to the
shifting blue surfaces of the harbour.

## 16

Late in the afternoon there were two knocks on the front door. Billyjim let go the kitchen-table leg he'd been swinging on and scampered away down the hall. Benton came up behind him as he wrestled with the big brass handle. It was the post boy, cap in one hand and an envelope in the other.

'Looks like another one to me, Mr Benton. Didn't see it come in but ...'

Since the beginning there'd been perhaps thirty. Benton could still feel the texture of each one between his fingers, could see the thirty front doors, the thirty front gates and the long slow streets that led up to them.

'You're still ...' the boy broke off. 'You're still delivering them, I suppose, I ...'

'Yes, Frank.'

'Well, better be off then.' And already he was darting across to his bicycle, glad to be freed of responsibility. Benton and Billyjim watched him wordlessly as he skimmed away downhill out of sight. Benton turned back into the drawing room, his son clambering up onto his lap as he sat down. Normally Benton would have hustled him back to the kitchen but this time he let the boy settle back against his chest as he ran a thumb under the flap of the envelope. The first, he knew, would begin as always: *PLEASE DELIVER ACCOMPANYING FATAL WAR CASUALTY TELEGRAM TO* ... and one more house would be singled out: *14 WATTLE STREET, 22 GIPPS ST*—and Benton would have the second windowed envelope, yellow in his inside pocket, to carry to its chosen door. Inside, as he knew from having it handed back to him on several occasions, were always the same words: *IT IS WITH DEEP REGRET THAT I HAVE TO INFORM YOU*

*THAT* (and here would follow the number, rank and name of the one singled out from ninety thousand) *HAS BEEN KILLED IN ACTION*, usually, though a few *DIED OF WOUNDS* or *DIED OF DISEASE ON* (and here the date—which tended to correlate, if you thought about it closely, with headlines such as *Major Allied Push: Counterattack Repelled*) *AND DESIRE TO CONVEY TO YOU THE PROFOUND SYMPATHY OF THE MINISTER FOR DEFENCE AND THE MILITARY BOARD.*

Maybe it was the form of words that did it: the way it left you useless in someone else's doorway or living room, searching for speech, impelled to reach out a comforting arm but not quite able. In the beginning Benton, like the rest, had managed his platitude or two: 'A man who dies in a just cause ... Then later and more lamely: 'Well, if there's anything I can do, Mrs ... He was a fine young man, I'm told.' To be followed by the quick about-turn down the steps and out the gate, feeling through the back of your skull the woman or father struck still in the doorway, holding in their hand, amazed, that random slip of yellow.

And this time, with Billyjim warm on his lap, there was simply:

> *MRS V. BENTON*
> *WALLAGUNDAH*
> *VIA GERADGERY*

For the first time and without thought Benton went straight ahead and tore it open. *1928 CORPORAL JOHN BENTON, KILLED IN ACTION, SEPTEMBER 10, 1916.* And once again Senator Pearce had seen fit to express his *PROFOUND SYMPATHY* and his *DEEP REGRET.*

Tomorrow would be soon enough. There were usually four days at least between the telegrams and the papers. What would this be in the *Herald*? List 206? And in the Armidale *Express* the compositor would widen his type a little to fit in one more name. Now, as he sat there staring out through the window at the formless grey finish of the afternoon and Billyjim began to wriggle plaintively away, Amy came in, unseen and questioning. As she sat down beside him on the sofa he passed the telegram silently to her.

## 17

By half past eight the next morning Benton was already flicking the bay mare northwards up the highway. Five miles north and ten miles west. Soon after he'd taken up the parish Benton had arranged with Coughlan, the carrier, to hire a sulky whenever he needed it—which was not too often; once every six weeks or so to Wallagundah and his mother; once in three months to one of the outlying private chapels on the last few original runs in the district. Benton, initially, had rather enjoyed these latter, so determinedly English, occasions with the magpies' ironic obbligato in a tree nearby or a roar from the bull paddock in the silence before the sermon. Or he had until he realised the double condescension involved, being as he was a virtual newcomer and, in some way not defined, an employee like any other.

One generation only at Wallagundah and its mere four thousand acres hadn't helped acceptance much either. Big enough for Lyall, he knew, and a couple of stockmen, but even then a deal of it was uncleared scrubby ridges, like the one you ultimately achieved on the way in, overlooking the homestead: a few white buildings scattered, a windbreak of pines and a plume of smoke. Though Benton had never begrudged his older and younger brothers their hard financial interest in the place, he still felt a slight unnameable ache each time he breasted that final rise and through the gap in the white-stemmed gums saw it all again spread out before him.

As yet, however, he was only three miles out of town. Two Fords a little while ago had rattled past him as if in tandem, not raising much dust, the dew still wet on the gravel. The day was shaping itself gently into a perfect denial of the night before—the sweaty wrestle with his nightmares, the naphtha flash of shells, the failing parries with rifle and bayonet in a monochrome landscape. Someone (Jack) had been moaning for help near the parapet just as he'd woken. God, in the wide-eyed aftermath of such things, seemed incurably distant.

He remembered staring at the ceiling and thinking, rather schematically, of Jack's soul; seeking for himself (and for his mother) that reassurance he himself had uttered in so many doorways and only a few months earlier had proffered from the pulpit. Heaven, for Benton, had always been difficult to visualise; to locate the impulsive and defiant Jack there was almost impossible. *In my house are many mansions* ... More relevant to Jack maybe was the last-minute thief beside Christ on the cross. Heaven, he knew, was something purely of the spirit, a tenuous paradise the Gospels never quite defined, something endless between the Watcher and the watched. Yes, it had been Jack out there while David had clung to the firestep, machine-gun fire raking the parapet, and somehow, cut in between Jack's moans, David could hear with a quite different clarity the jibes of their last real argument, David home for a week from St John's and Jack up from school.

'Prig.'

Jack's word it had been, on loan from a friend, and used not so much of David himself but for the high church chaplain who'd been David's mentor.

'I wouldn't say that,' David had said, half-ashamed of his moderation.

'Well, you're no better yourself. And that's where you got it after all.'

'What do you mean?'

'All this love of prancing about, even the way you put out a candle; such a serious business, with snuffer and all.'

'Well, it's just ...'

'Just priggishness, I'd say. If you lot were bloody genuine you'd sell all that real estate and give it to the natives, in India or somewhere—a more likely place for the second coming anyway, I'd reckon.' David could remember Jack pausing and staring into the fire. It had been the May holidays, their mother asleep already down the hall. 'Not that your "Creeping Jesus" friend gave us much of a second chance last year when he caught us coming back from Jenkins' orchard. The Gaffer himself would have let us off with six on the arse but the Reverend Smarm had to press right on with the homilies till the poor old bugger would practically have expelled us just to give himself some peace.'

The exchange was randomly salted with gunfire and even in retrospect David still winced at the language. The syllable 'prig' had continued in his ears as he awoke and echoed even now in the bay mare's hooves clipping the gravel.

Relations, to David's relief, had improved considerably from then on: Jack growing into a measure of tolerance as the world revealed more important shortcomings; David slipping more into the mundanity of his parish and the saving straightforwardness of Amy. By the time Jack caught the train south after the news from Gallipoli had been coming in, David was genuinely distressed to see him go and Jack, at that point, held nothing against his brother for staying.

Benton, four miles out now, pushed the memories away and let the morning paddocks filter in, the granite outcrops, the scattered trees. A few sheep were working along the fence and lifted their heads as he passed. He pondered their half-human faces and thought of the relish with which Barker and his dean employed the image of the shepherd and his flock. That one on the end had a touch of Mrs Giddins somehow, or was it a judge in full regalia bemused by a difficult case? This vicar in his sulky, midweek, mid-morning, from nowhere, to nowhere? Benton imagined the leisurely operations of a sheep's brain, which he also rather enjoyed bread-crumbed and fried on Sunday evenings.

But as he reached the turn-off and headed down the Long

Flat Road it was his mother he was thinking of. He, at least, had
had a day to get used to it, a year in some ways. She, Benton
knew, had never permitted herself any precise knowledge
of what was really happening. Jack would contrive somehow
(without actually being ungallant) to be some headquarters'
orderly or find a safe spot in transport somewhere. The jokiness
of his letters seemed to confirm this, even though the papers
were sometimes quite specific about what the Second Division
had been up to.

Years before, as the two older sons moved away—Lyall
into his own dour competence on the place and David to his
training at St John's—the mother had drawn the last one closer.
Jack had been brought home from school a year early (Violet
and the masters agreeing that, given his attitude, it was hardly
worthwhile keeping him on to the senior year). He'd almost
had to fend his mother off and insist on going out with Lyall,
despite their shortness with each other, for the mustering and
crutching. Jack, secretly and against all the evidence, seemed
to believe he was marked out for something better than four
thousand family acres. 'Big dreams, eh boy?' Benton could
remember Lyall saying, when he said anything, before taxing
Jack with an unshut gate. David himself had gone out with
them as recently as the summer of 1914 and been distinctly
disappointed. As the three of them had ridden down the long
slope to the homestead after a long day David, waiting for some
sense of three-fold camaraderie, even if unspoken, could hardly
decide from which of them he felt the more distant.

As he opened the gate and turned at last onto Benton land,
David had the whole four of them convened in his head, an
uneasy snapshot: dead father, dead brother, and the two there
waiting now. In the suspension of his three-hour journey in the
sulky the war had receded; the gap between Frizelle and Barker
had stretched till it disappeared in the tilting horizons. Then,
breasting the final ridge, he saw the white buildings (homestead,
stables, barn, dairy and meathouse with a shearing shed off to

the right) all spread out below him just as they should be on such a morning, a soak a little way up the slope behind the house giving back the light.

As he stepped onto the veranda boards, Benton felt again the yellow message on his chest, an audible crinkle. Though the dogs were still yelping on their chains away there to the right beside the stables, his mother did not come out. Normally, with Amy and Billyjim on a weekend, the two kelpies would long since have brought her to the gate but today, midweek, there was no sign. He knocked once on the green painted door; then, as he was about to knock again, it swung back and she was standing there, a lean, tall woman not much shorter than her son. She had only to look him once in the face to see what it was. She seemed to shiver, as if about to collapse on his shoulder, but instead waved him through to the kitchen. The heat of the stove and the smell of cupcakes (Lyall was a man of small weaknesses) filled the room. 'Telegram,' she said tonelessly and without looking back as she slid a kettle onto a burner.

'Yesterday afternoon,' said David, pulling a chair out from the table. He put the telegram down on the bare surface between them. 'I thought I'd better ...' She slipped the message without comment from its opened envelope, read it twice (Benton could count off the words as she did so—*IT IS WITH DEEP REGRET* ...); then folded it back in its cover.

'Lyall's just over in the Creek Paddock. Should be home for lunch.' Violet Benton at that moment seemed no less further off from him than any other woman who'd received the same news at his hands. He wanted to reach across the table and grab her delicate shoulders but could not do so. As her son, as a vicar, there should be something to say. He could hear as he sat there with unwelcome clarity the standard phrases ('You shouldn't let it hurt too much, Mrs Benton' ... 'He was a fine man, I'm told.'). He could imagine Barker or Denning-Jones, his dean, saying something like that with verve almost. His own helpless silence was surely less cruel. For one moment she looked as if she might unfold towards him across the table but then the kettle whistled and she got up to make the tea, shaking two teaspoons in, then tipping scalding water (mercilessly, it had seemed to him as a child) on top of it. With the tea caddied and drawing, she looked at him once more across the table. 'And what does God say, Davey?'

The Bentons, much to David's chagrin at one point, were a Christmas and Easter family only. David's vocation had always mildly amazed them (and angered Jack). Twice a year, and no more (David's father must have thought), would put the church in perspective. David had been wondering, too, whether or not she and Lyall knew what had been happening at St Jude's. Though only fifteen miles out it was quite probable that, even after two weeks, Lyall still didn't know. He was not a man who could only make it home via the saloon bar at the Royal. Even if he did know, he'd probably spared Violet.

'Not what he's supposed to, I'm afraid,' said David at last. 'About us, or the Germans, if it comes to that.' Though her question had been ironic it was not irony, Benton saw now with regret, that she'd wanted back. Surely there was something there beyond the twice-a-year proprieties and all that doctrine? *This is a hard saying. Who can hear it, Love your enemies, do good to them which hate you.* His mother's clear grey eyes had not flinched though they trembled a little at the edges. 'I'm sorry, mother,' he said, reaching out a hand at last across the bare surface of the table. 'It's hard enough with the others but with you ...' Her hand was hard, thin, cool and still somehow parental. Despite the differences in time it seemed that the telegram's swinging blow had caught them both simultaneously and these clasped hands and the beginnings of tears were all that could be said.

The mare took it slowly, propping a little, down the shadowed cutting. His mother, as Lyall would probably say later, had 'taken it pretty well'; Amy no doubt would have lasted out the

night but not without some worry, especially after the stones
of last Friday evening, and between Lyall and his mother there
was a sufficiency now, albeit wordless, which David knew he
couldn't add to. His brother had come in for lunch as she'd said
and, seeing the mid-week sulky, dismounted at the gate and had
not needed to be told. Taking off his hat and wiping his feet,
Lyall had suddenly filled the doorway and, not even nodding to
David, had, in perhaps the only spontaneous gesture of his adult
life, taken his mother in his arms as she rose up weightlessly
from the kitchen chair.

As it turned out Lyall hadn't heard about the sermon. His
few acquaintances were not noted church-goers and those who
knew may have wished to spare him. Certainly, thought David,
as the sulky once more neared the turn-off, today would hardly
have been the day to bring it up. His mother would puzzle a
little over his listless 'Not what he's supposed to' but that would
fade in the grief ahead. It was an uncomfortable gap, even so,
that Benton could feel widening between the buried soldier
(hero, as Barker would have it) and the living pacifist (or coward
as Winters would no doubt be phrasing it by now). One day,
perhaps soon, the two back there at Wallagundah might see it
David's way—but not yet.

Coming at last into the evening lamps and levelled smoke
of kitchen fires, Benton sensed again the dimensions of the
courage he was going to need. So much of this fortnight
had been predictable: Somerton's choir, the tennis club, the
Women's Guild of Mrs Giddins, rumours about the Parish
Council, the thinness of his own voice in the half-empty church.
Only the bishop's silence stood outside the pattern, a leisurely
gavel waiting to fall. The bay mare quickened its pace now and
turned, without instruction, left into Coughlan's stables.

Later that same night with Amy waiting for him in bed down
the hall (he could see her brown hair released on the pillows,
the Dickens novel in her hand), Benton sat in the drawing room

staring into the empty fireplace attempting to pray, or at least to order his thoughts. Only at that moment with his mother had the fact of Jack's death truly reached him, carried by wire twelve thousand miles, delayed in its impact, but finally now recorded. As if one more New Englander, confusion in his heart and all about him, wrapped in an army blanket and tipped into French soil, could ultimately make a difference. Winnowed away from New South Wales, the whole of the Second Division seemed poised on the lips of similarly pointless holes—or had already found them. And yet if that chaplain Watkins was right, it was all still a matter of faith, faith in something (though not in Jack's case, God), a faith that saved you for a time from madness.

Whatever it was, Benton knew that his brother would have seen what he was embarked on now as the surest betrayal. There was no thought further about Jack's immortal soul or its possible destination. The Western Front, as Benton saw it in reports and in his dreams, seemed to have cancelled both destinations—and the souls that might have gone to either. God, it was obvious to Benton now as he stared at the dead carbons of the fireplace, had long ago lost interest. Christ was simply a physical being located earlier in time but still integrity's final test; Arius's human Christ—but with his God subtracted. Jack would not have understood but in some eternity, of which Benton had by no means lost the habit, their parallels would meet. And still there could be no accounting.

As if finally freed to do so Benton roughed out in his mind the telegram for Mr Jeremy Frizelle, teacher, pacifist, ex-priest, of 14 Langlee Ave, Waverley. He shuffled the epithets in his hand. It almost amused him to think of Barker and Frizelle in the same room. Had that been why Frizelle had left? Some Sydney equivalent of Barker back before the war? He remembered those pre-war circulars from the Peace Society which he'd so haughtily ignored. 'Peace Sunday' indeed. It had sounded so fatuous. *PREPARED TO HELP IN ANY WAY POSSIBLE*, the telegram would run. *PLEASE ADVISE.*

Bearing it to the post office at ten the next morning Benton was aware now of a change in the distances. Ever since he'd come to the town, to the vicarage, there'd been the normal distances suited to newcomers. Having a property fifteen miles out was not enough; the Benton name out there was barely twenty years old anyway. Though the town itself had been there only sixty years, you had to be second generation at least to count. Anyone else was a parvenu, half-expected to move on anytime. There was that other distance too, given by the collar: his own congregation nodding politely, the other persuasions shifting their eyes at the final moment, knowing who he was but not yielding the point. Storekeepers, he noticed, were friendly enough; they had their own reasons.

But now in this gusty September morning there was distance of another kind: heads that turned away at twenty paces instead of the usual one; unseeing silences overtaking those who only a month ago would have given that time of day his position required. Once or twice only did he catch a rueful, secret smile from some fettler perhaps, or stationhand, never seen before.

Under the store verandas and in the windows the campaign for the 28th had already begun. Elder Smiths had a big *VOTE YES* right next to their *THE EMPIRE NEEDS YOU* and *GOD BLESS DADDY* posters. Benton had half expected the *VOTE YES* posters to be as ubiquitous as Captain Winters' had been back in May, but this time they were plastered on veranda posts only and any spare surfaces that didn't too clearly have an owner. The shopkeepers, Benton detected, were not so keen to declare themselves. A few fairly crude *VOTE NOs* were already being slapped up on top of their rivals (Bert Spenser's work, no

doubt). There was a *VOTE NO* too on the Hibernian wall but
maybe the manager hadn't seen it yet. It was only ten o'clock,
after all.

If the townspeople hadn't yet taken up their positions, they
were at least, Benton realised, facing the inevitability of having
to do so. There were possibly less than half a dozen activists
on either side but they would be sufficient. The reluctantly
abandoned simplicities of August '14 were giving away to
something else, not quite visible yet but due to appear by the
28th. Frizelle, he knew, would be pleased to get the telegram,
and Benton in turn was relieved to have it forcing him beyond
the half-measures more natural to him. Everything around him
now was bearing down on the 28th—there was no chance at all
of breaking back, nor, he was glad to discover, did he have any
wish to do so.

The outsize, polished granite pillars of Geradgery Post Office
always seemed to humble the mere brick behind them, an
oddness Benton had often pondered. It was Mrs Giddins, finally,
who had told him the town story of an architect's mistake down
in Sydney. The building seemed, he'd sometimes thought, to
symbolise the town: the pillars the few first families, those
big runs; the small bricks crouched behind them that lack of
follow-through. As he came to the steps Benton noticed at the
kerb a young man sitting at the wheel of a car in conversation
with another leaning down from a horse. They stopped, almost
as if he'd been the topic of their talk, and watched him as he
mounted the steps. Both, he saw, wore houndstooth sportscoats.
He could see the scorn now on the face of the one in the car
which itself was clean, foursquare, prosperous, an Oldsmobile,
perhaps, from the *Bulletin* advertisements.

'Well, there goes one Boche,' said the horseman. 'What do
you reckon, Barry?' Or so Benton thought he heard. In a couple
of quick looks stopping short of a stare, he couldn't really
recognise either of them. The one behind the wheel might just
be a McEwan though—there'd been that christening four years

back. Could that youth so grandly seated there be the same petulant thirteen year old up from school for the weekend to see the last of his siblings named?

'Oh, I wouldn't say that, mate,' said the one in the car. 'Takes a bit of guts to be a Hun, you know, especially when you've got the whole damn British Empire to deal with ... or most of it, anyway.' Benton, with the distance and the wind, picked up the key words only—their looks filled in the rest. What else could you do but ignore them? They'd be gone soon enough, it seemed—whichever way it went on the 28th. He strode through the pillars and into a smallish room, a counter on one side, a writing bench on the other. He began to scratch Frizelle's address on the form.

When he came out they were still there, staring. As many had done already to him this morning, Benton looked straight through them and set off southwards up the street. There was something harder to be done.

*CYRIL SOMERTON—NEWSAGENT AND STATIONER*. And ex-choirmaster, Benton added to himself, pausing at a poster which exactly filled a panel of the door. Two men, one in civilian spats, the other an officer, confronted each other, the latter a fraction taller and more suave. *You boast of your freedom*, he said, *come and fight for it*. Benton pushed back the door. A small bell sounded. Somerton, halfway along the counter, looked up from a paper and stiffened, much as Benton had done on seeing him there. It was a narrow shop, somewhat understocked, with a row of war maps pinned to the wall.

'Morning, Cyril.'

'Good morning,' said Somerton, not yielding a name.

'Still got the bushmen's bible?' The jocularity surprised Benton himself as much as Somerton who walked without comment along behind the counter; then stooped to pick up a *Bulletin* and came back. What did the bushmen think of it these days anyway? It looked as if, despite the rift, Somerton had deliberately kept one aside for him.

'You know,' Somerton began, 'it's a pity, I must say, but ...'

'I think I know how you feel,' said Benton, reaching for his coins. 'Though it has left a gap. I can't pretend ...'

'It's not just because of the others, you know.'

'I know,' Benton said, wanting to ease the other man's discomfort. 'Could be the least of our problems in the next few weeks, I suspect.' He handed over his one and six and, as Somerton very deliberately rang it up, drifted towards the door. Benton's half-embarrassed smile back over his shoulder as the bell rang again seemed to cut something short in the newsagent's mouth. Some kind of rapprochement? But already Benton was outside and heading up the street again.

On the final two blocks near the church and lifting his gaze towards Bald Knob, Benton felt again that dampness on his collar, in his armpits—a sweat not so much from exertion or weather but of the nerves. The morning sun, three-quarters high, floated there benevolently enough on his shoulder, the wind brought smells of flowering trees tumbling over the gardens. Tree of Heaven? That was one of the few he knew; that conjunction of the physical and metaphysical ... Amy was the one for plants. The distances back there, the distances of the morning, were blurring and merging, threatening a little less. Sometimes on a day like this, and not just because of his tallness, Benton felt closer to the clouds than to the gravel which crackled remotely under his shoes. Somewhere, far back, lessened by perspective, were two youths sneering, one in an open car, the other leaning forward from his horse.

'Please, sir, did you see this about your brother?'

The rest of the class had shot straight out. Three or four, as if by arrangement, had stayed behind and clustered around Benton by the door. The one called Douglas was thrusting a newsclipping at him. 'It was in the morning paper. Looks like you a bit.' Benton stooped and took up the defiant sepia smile, the same one which topped the piano at Wallagundah. It challenged you to disapprove. Always, out there, David's glance would slip along quickly: onto the father's photo, simplified by death, and Lyall's taken in his last year at school—as if a full-grown adult had been talked into a school uniform for some joke he didn't understand.

'Yes,' said Benton, not looking at them, 'that's my brother. He was killed a week ago.' As the children jostled and nudged each other below him he read the caption. *Cpl J. Benton was killed in action near Pozières, France, on I September. He was the son of Mrs Violet Benton and the late Mr William Benton, of Wallagundah, via Geradgery. Cpl Benton's older brother continues to run the family property; his second brother, the Rev. David Benton, is rector of St Jude's, Geradgery. Cpl Benton was an old boy of The Armidale School and is well-remembered by the masters there as a promising athlete and all-round sportsman.*

'I'm sorry, sir,' said Douglas as Benton handed back the clipping. The children filed out, gratified—except for the little girl with the brother 'somewhere in France'. Rosemary Steggart. He remembered the tone as much as the face.

'My grandpa says I shouldn't go to your class. He said to tell Mr McPhee not to let me go.'

'Oh, why was that?' said Benton. 'You're Church of England, aren't you?'

'Yes,' she said, 'but he says that a man like you ought to know better. He reckons you want the Kaiser to win ... and that it's a disgrace to the church.' Though she was still parroting, Benton saw, it was not just the secondhand insolence of a month ago ('Call 'em all up, he says.'). She seemed less certain now, as if she would have liked Benton to deny it, or at least explain. He glanced out across the playground, damp with the spring rains and scattered with groups of children tugging at each other, screaming and running.

'Well, Rosemary, he's probably thinking of some talks I've been giving lately about peace.' He looked down into her incomprehension. 'It's true I don't want the war to go on a minute longer than it has to—and that we should do whatever small thing we can to stop it. That doesn't mean I want the Germans to win.' The girl, Benton could see, was finding this hard to follow. 'A war doesn't have to be won to be stopped, you know. You just ask your grandfather what he thinks Jesus would have done.' He surprised himself with the past conditional; it would have been the present tense not so long ago. Looking down at Rosemary's face, an unresolved half-moon tilted up at him, he said with some asperity: 'Yes, Rosemary, you ask him when you get home what he thinks Christ would have done.' And leaving her standing there, he walked off to the little staffroom at the end of the veranda.

As Benton came in the other two teachers looked up, nodded vaguely and resumed some last-minute marking. McPhee himself seemed friendly, even solicitous. 'How's it going? They can be devils sometimes, that lot—not bad with a firm hand though.' He handed Benton the usual black tea.

'No trouble really,' said Benton.

'Sorry to hear about your brother,' McPhee said, reaching for the sugar. 'I saw it this morning, in the paper.'

'Yes,' said Benton distantly, as much to himself as to the headmaster. 'Had to tell my mother on Tuesday.'

'Hasn't changed your ... I've noticed it tends to one way or another.'

'No, not really,' said Benton. 'They don't all have to die.' He pondered his tea, a black pool in its thick, white, government cup. McPhee looked down also.

'You know, we've had a bit of trouble about you. Old Steggart's been in, young Rosemary's grandfather, used to be on the council years ago. He'd heard about your talk at the railway and threatened to report me to head office if I keep on letting you take R.I.' McPhee paused and smiled slightly. Benton noted the mild dishevelment of his tie and found himself liking the man, or wanting to. 'Seems to think you're out to destroy the war-effort singlehanded ... and a menace to young children, to boot. Not that I took any notice, mind you. It'll be a while yet before I let the grandpas in to run my school.'

Benton realised again that he had never quite known where McPhee stood, either before or after his own turnabout. Even now with this dismissal of old Steggart it was hard to tell but, sensing sympathy (or needing it), Benton was tempted to a confidence. 'If Steggart were the biggest problem, I wouldn't be too worried. There's the Parish Council, though. The bishop's a rather weightier case, I suspect.' He smiled at his own joke, picturing that notable continuum of chest and belly, the purple ground, the movements of that brazen cross. 'And not very pleased, I imagine, though I've yet to hear officially.' He looked out through a small window over the street: a row of weatherboard cottages, the convex corrugated-iron curling over verandas; hydrangeas and dahlias, and on the damp gravel nothing moving. 'Bit strange around town, too, of course, but I guess I'll just have to bear with that.' Suddenly Benton was tempted to mention the stones of last Friday night but saw it would not be welcome. He had gone too far already. The man's sympathy stopped neatly at the edge of his employment. He had no intention of being caught up in anything that would risk that. Benton scraped back his chair, got up and put his cup back on the sink. He felt rather than saw the other two look up briefly from their books. 'Yes, well, thanks anyway. See you next week then.'

'Yes. Fine,' said McPhee a little obscurely into his tea, as though a week might be quite a long time.

By the following Thursday, as McPhee had implied, a great deal had happened. Home Service call-up notices had been up for three days and the papers were already reporting the flurry of exemptions sought. *ALL MEN*, it declared on the wall of the post office, *WHO ON THE SECOND DAY OF OCTOBER, 1916, ARE OF THE AGE OF TWENTY-ONE YEARS AND UPWARDS AND UNDER THIRTY-FIVE YEARS WHO ARE UNMARRIED OR WIDOWERS WITHOUT CHILDREN ARE TO ENLIST AND SERVE AS REQUIRED*. Benton himself was doubly exempted, both as cleric and father. Prime Minister Hughes, a month home from the chiefs of staff—and English duchesses (as Spenser would probably point out)—was rounding up his Big Battalions against the day of the great approval. Older brothers, younger brothers, were being forced to report even though (as Benton knew was the case with several of his congregation) a family conference a year or more before had made its own decisions. As the clamour for exemptions mounted, Benton could almost smile at the official frustration: so many reasons— this headmaster irreplaceable, that man his sick mother's only support, this man the only son to run a farm. He could almost wince for Winters too, the indignity of it—a young G.P.S. headmaster successfully wriggling free, those thousands of small-town eligibles fading away in a haze of excuses. Not that the magistrates were acceding to them all but the whole call-up, even if only for Home Service, was clearly, Benton saw, a prelude to the wider consequence of 28 October. It was something that Frizelle and Spenser could both oppose in their different ways and yet be strangely grateful for as well. Heaven-sent, as Frizelle would not quite say.

And in the meantime Benton continued his diminished rounds, including some visits to the very old who only just recalled the August declaration two years gone and seemed to have lost all interest in it since. To have this clerical young man stooping politely in their doorway was still a pleasant punctuation in the week. And one young man of his absentee congregation, Benton learned, had enlisted since the sermon, forgoing his church farewell. A marriage in the parish, planned six months before, went ahead anyway, for better or for worse; a thirty-year-old farmer up near Ben Lomond and the young daughter of McPhillamy, the grain and hides merchant. Attendance on Sunday had levelled off at a third and Benton, sensing tolerance, if not agreement, did not feel the need to urge an instant peace or a NO on the 28th.

He had even managed, one clear October Tuesday, another drive out to Wallagundah, this time with Amy and Billyjim, and was gratified to see that his mother was indeed 'holding up well', as Lyall put it—or could manage what passed for this in front of visitors. Seeing her more closely Benton felt she might almost have been waiting for some further telegram to confirm the first. Lyall, just over thirty-five, was not threatened by the call-up and had no need to plead his 'aged mother'. It was clear, though, that the threat to his few younger acquaintances had had its effect. But if he knew anything of his brother's sermon he gave no sign. Sitting there on the veranda, one riding boot propped on the toe of another, Lyall was even quieter than usual while Amy, the emotional first moments past, talked intermittently of Billyjim who tumbled happily among the shrubs in front of them, wheeling back every now and again towards his mother. Between her son and daughter-in-law Violet Benton sat frailly, seeming somehow to have mislaid, like a pair of spectacles, the secret of that easy chatter with Amy which had filled out previous visits. And long before the sun got down towards the skyline David, oppressed by his own irrelevance, had loaded his family into the sulky for the long drive back. They could have stayed—his mother suggested it—and nothing in Geradgery required him next morning—but David felt already the long road back in his wrists: the first outward cutting up and over the ridge, the Long Flat Road (the green to pale-grey paddocks either side), the ten miles of the highway south to Geradgery, verandas caught by the last light.

Finally, with a blanket across their knees and Billyjim passed out on Amy's lap, they reached the first houses in exactly that light which Benton had imagined, and passed through, despite the bay mare's attempt to dodge left into Coughlan's stables, directly to St Jude's. Half a dozen streetlamps on the way served merely to outline the town's emptiness. A few silhouettes showed in the Royal and Hibernian doorways. In the window of Norton's Café three or four faces did not look up from their plates. They did not need to for Benton to feel that collective opinion and feel how the blanket across the six knees of his family measured its triple involvement, unsought or otherwise. At the vicarage he dropped off Amy and Billyjim and let the mare have her head back to the stables. The four blocks home again on foot always seemed to lift him slightly; his land legs finding their way again. The newness of those early stars and their distances seemed to free him a little from the tightening he felt around him. The bishop could hardly let things run much longer and, if he did, this rally for Frizelle in Sydney must be the final word.

In the post as he came in were two letters. Pausing on the veranda he glanced at them by the slit of light from above the front door but the writing and, in one case, type, revealed nothing. Normally he would have waited but on the half-lit way to the kitchen he already had the first one, strangely weightless, open. It was a single white feather, a White Leghorn's with a yellowish point, complete with a folded sheet of paper on which in childish print was scrawled FROM ALL OF THOSE WHO HAD THE GUTS TO GO. It was something he'd been expecting for weeks and, in a sense, for two years. His calling, he knew, was a kind of insulation—against that cowardice of the flesh that would not risk itself to shrapnel; against that cowardice of the spirit which could not say no to the unison of those who'd gone and those who'd never need to. A minister could step neatly aside from both—which rather explained, Benton had since realised, a great deal of what got spoken from the pulpit in the first weeks of the war—and since. Not too many of those *who had the guts to go* had as yet returned. Athol Dalby, Winters' recruiting sergeant, and the disaffected Wally Tippet were the only two he knew of and for different reasons he couldn't imagine either of them having done it. Dalby, if his speech at Winters' rally were any guide, was too straightforward and, in his own way, honourable. Proud relatives were a more likely bet: the father grandly sending his son's letters to the *Express*; the sister tired of knitting Red Cross socks, and not quite letting herself wonder why; maybe even Mrs Giddins—but that was unfair. Or was it? Again he imagined her badgering the hapless Somerton over his morning paper. The bishop, if slow to move, was always well informed, one way or another. Mrs Giddins, Benton guessed, had at least that much to answer for. Outside the kitchen door he twisted the feather in his fingers and slipped it into his pocket.

The second letter, typed, needed a stronger light. Amy, finalising some cold meat and potato salad, looked up at him with a tired smile. Benton, not yet sitting down and sensing her clairvoyance, began to read. The letterhead would have been enough in itself but with a flat curiosity he read on anyway, imagining as he did so Barker's orotund dictation, Miss Pym's notebook on her knee.

*My dear Benton,*

*Having regard to your obstinate and repeated efforts to undermine the confidence of your parishioners and others in this great Christian struggle I have, in view of certain complaints from the Parish Council,*

*no option but to withdraw for an indefinite period your licence to
officiate in my diocese.*

*In consideration for your good wife, on whom I imagine you
have already visited much needless distress, I have asked the Parish
Council to continue your stipend for another month by which time
I shall have arranged for you to be replaced by a man of genuine
Christian courage and conviction.*

*Yours etc.
Barker*

When he'd finished Amy reached out across the table and
wordlessly took the letter from him. The message, in essence,
had been on its way for weeks; only its phrasing had been in
doubt and, given Barker's feeling for histrionics, even that could
have been roughly predicted.

'Well,' she said, pulling out her chair to sit down, 'it might
just have been worse, I suppose. Nice of him to think of me.
Needless distress indeed.' Seeing the sturdy quality of her
irritation Benton felt his own anxiety recede a little, though
not his anger with Barker's resounding self-assurance. *A man
of genuine Christian courage and conviction.* It seemed to stick
sideways in the throat. How could the man be reading the same
Gospels? Where did Christ fit in exactly? Was Jesus himself the
man to lead yet another assault on the German line in the quest
for 'Christian values'? Or could that be left to Haig, 'every inch
a soldier, from the neck down', as the saying had begun to have
it? He pulled out his chair and sat down, feeling his anger fade a
little as he did so. A long sadness began to replace it. Even with
his faith so altered it was as if, with these instructions, the whole
Anglican liturgy and all it had come to mean to him had been
taken away with no hope of return. The example, the teachings,
of Christ had led him to this point; now everything except that
figure, all the textures and resonance of his faith and practice,
were sliding away, leaving just that single image, that example,

lonely, stripped, one-dimensional perhaps, but sufficient. Benton had never been more certain that the continuance of the war, *this great blood-spilling business*, as Hughes termed it, could never be justified. Nothing Barker might threaten from his huge and episcopal mahogany desk would alter that. It was a matter of compromise, of coming to one's senses. Even now, two years too late, that jigsaw, those interlocked simplicities of that first six weeks leading to Britain's declaration, must be seen as the mistake it had been and finally disowned.

He looked at the sliced mutton with some appetite. Without grace they began to eat in silence. And in the short term, thought Benton, smiling again across at Amy but not really seeing her, there was the 28th. Australia, the only combatant with no death penalty for desertion, might also be the first to knock back conscription, the process by which the guns were fed. In Geradgery the alliance to bring this about was, Benton knew, somewhat grotesque and distinctly uncomfortable. Even had he been gregarious by nature Spenser and Tippet would hardly have been the first of his friends. But it was a beginning even so. Other stranger, more hopeful things might happen right across the country, across France, across Russia, across Germany ... Meanwhile the lists kept coming in. List No. 208, List No. 209. Pozières was over for the time being, but Haig and Joffre were up to something—that much at least was coming through the papers. Hard to say how many thousands exactly. You could perhaps count up the names; the figures were never published. There would be time for more before year's end. And those who'd buried Jack would in their turn be buried.

Benton's reply to the bishop's letter did not take written form. By seven fifteen the next morning he was already across the other side of town knocking at the door of the skewed weatherboard cottage Spenser had given as his address. A few pullets had scattered as he'd lifted a latch and swung back the gate. At the second knock a slight, washed-out woman with dressing gown and undone hair edged her face around the door. And saw the collar.

'There's not been an ...' He might have been bringing a telegram.

'No, Mrs Spenser, I just wanted to see Bert. Thought I might catch him before ...'

'No luck, reverend. He's on the early shift this week—starts at six sharp.' She looked blankly into his face and kept the door where it was. He could see now why she didn't know. Just another detail Spenser hadn't told her. 'What did you—he's not one of yours, you know. Used to be a Catholic when I first met him.' She opened the door a little. 'Long time now since he saw the insides of a church!' she said, smiling for the first time. Benton could see she was no more than forty. 'Inside of a pub more likely, should be home by five though—if he doesn't stop off too long at the Hibernian.' It was as if some cheap colour had freshened her face. She finally swung back the door. 'Cup of tea, reverend? Usually have one about now.'

'No thanks, Mrs Spenser. Just tell Bert I was here about the campaign. He'll know what I mean!'

'Ah, that,' she said, beginning to understand.

'I'll come over at five then, if that's all right.'

'I'll tell him,' she agreed dully.

Halfway down the block, heading for the viaduct and his own side of town, Benton glanced back and saw her still there, a faded grey blur at the veranda rail.

At Cyril Somerton's on the way home Benton, his first customer, bought the previous day's *Herald* (in a functional silence preferred by both) and, back at the vicarage, having cut a little wood for Amy, settled down in the drawing room to read the latest accounts of the meetings in Sydney. Even in these muffled outlines he could conjure for himself the gatherings of either side: the respectable meetings in respectable halls (*We loyal citizens of the Anti-German League pledge ourselves to heartily support by every means in our power, the referendum proposals of the Prime Minister*); and the rowdier ones elsewhere as Alderman X was counted out and howled down by Sinn Feiners, I.W.W., shirkers and renegades and *a section at the back who would not stand for 'God Save the King'*. The report of the latter made them seem motley indeed and instinctively he drew back from their methods. Even at school Benton had always disliked interjection and the making of scenes. As a preacher he knew he was spoiled by the deferential silence into which his words passed for consideration. Yet a man was entitled to be heard out; it pained him to be in league with the footshufflers and hecklers. But the vision now of those other meetings pained him even more: several hundred grey or shiny heads intent on a stage with Union Jack and a man delivering the platitudes espoused by Barker into a fervent silence, broken only by a few 'Hear, hears'. *This meeting regards the voting in favour of conscription on 28 October as a humane, patriotic and religious duty.* And those already volunteered were dying meanwhile as Haig looked still for his breakthrough of the year. The turbulence of Pozières made that of the hecklers mild indeed.

He looked out the window at the burgeoning, midmorning elms but it was the meeting in the Domain, just ten days off, that rose into focus. Already he could feel the turmoil, the human whirlpools as the fights broke out, the perimeter of policeman and on the left the view away over the Botanic Gardens to the harbour and Kirribilli. Frizelle had wanted him as a practising parson but he might be even more effective now. 'I now call upon the Rev. David Benton, until recently rector of St Jude's in the diocese of Armidale. Unfortunately in his search for peace and in his rejection of conscription Mr Benton has been forbidden by his bishop to administer the sacraments for which he was ordained. Ladies and gentlemen, a man of both courage and conviction, Mr David Benton.' It was a neat reversal of Barker's phrase but Benton as yet had nothing to follow it. Maybe Frizelle and his friends in the Peace Society would see him as less valuable now and let the whole thing slide. Either way, Benton now realised, Barker had forced him to a further commitment; sermons in St Jude's now could never be enough, anyway. The referendum, the peace, had to be taken into the streets. To do this in Geradgery and not be labelled a crank he needed Spenser—and anyone else they could muster between them. To judge from the main street now, the forces for conscription were having it all their own way. For people like Cyril Somerton or the shire president, Ned McLennan, to vote *YES* was synonymous with the respectability they either sought or feared to lose.

But some things at least, Benton saw, were pushing in the other direction. The Home Service call-up exemption lists were telling their own story. The threat after all was still twelve thousand miles away from Australian farms, and this project dear to the little Welshman was proving downright inconvenient to families who had long since made their own covenant with the war, deciding family by family who should go and who should not. Stockmen and labourers were not coming any cheaper either.

*And keep Australia white* ... That was another line which helped. Benton had seen it in the *Herald* and heard it once or twice locally. It was not an argument he greatly liked (would

Christ himself be sufficiently wan?) but it was more effective than many. The Maltese, Spenser no doubt would say, were the edge of the wedge. Yet whiteness, he knew, could work both ways. Let the Royal Navy go by some mischance to the bottom of the North Sea (the damage at Jutland was heavy enough), and the hordes would be here by the end of next week. It was an image which, despite the celestial smiles of laundrymen and market gardeners, could still send a shiver up the spine.

'Not to mention the Irish,' said Bert Spenser, six hours later in his tiny kitchen. 'They might have thought those Pearse and Connolly fellers last Easter were pretty half-baked, guns from the Huns and all that, but when they started shooting 'em once a week, that changed things a bit. There's not so many'll die for the old England now—especially if they get no say in it—as they won't if Billy has his way.' Mrs Spenser hovered over their shoulders, not quite shelling her peas and not quite listening either. At the door she'd suggested they use the front parlour but Spenser, seeming not to have heard, led his man straight through to the kitchen where they now sat awkwardly under her elbows. With a union man, Benton saw, it might have been different. He would have liked to ask her to join them, but could see how impossible this would be even if there were another chair. 'And the worst thing of all is bloody Hughes himself trying to bring it in. A Labor prime minister—though you wouldn't have thought so in the English papers apparently. A genuine Labor rat. They use the movement to give themselves a leg up then wave their mates goodbye.' Spenser paused and took up his cup of tea. 'Well, what do you reckon, David? Might as well call you that now the bishop's got it in for you, eh?'

Benton winced. The friendliness was almost snide. 'The moral argument's a good one, I think,' he said at last. 'Not too many women are keen to condemn another mother's son to kill or be killed. They seem to know what it's about even if the fathers don't.' He fiddled with his cup and thought of some of the send-offs he'd presided over, the mother at the edge of tears, the father as proud at the moment of departure as he'd been when they'd brought the boy in, squalling, eighteen years before.

'Yeah,' said Spenser, 'to see some of them it makes you wonder.' He suddenly reached out and started to ransack a Manila package that lay between them on the table. 'Hang on a moment.' Benton watched him haul out several posters and thought of at least one that wouldn't be there—that new one up on Somerton's door with *I didn't raise my son to be a soldier*: on one side a dapper little creature cringing away from his stentorian mother and on the other, *I'm proud I did*, with a lady whose son, capped and epauletted, stared away dutifully to the European horizon. 'Yeah, here it is,' said Spenser at last. 'This ought to do it if anything will.' He started to read in a voice so bathetic that Benton suspected, wrongly, that he was not serious.

> *Why is your face so white, mother?*
> *Why do you choke for breath?*
> *Oh, I have dreamt in the night, my son,*
> *That I doomed a man to death.*
>
> *They gave me a ballot paper,*
> *The grim death warrant of doom,*
> *And I surely sentenced the man to death*
> *In that dreadful little room.*

Benton said nothing. 'What do you reckon?' Spenser inquired with some enthusiasm. 'That'd be something you could use; finish up with maybe.' Again Benton didn't quite hear; he was looking at Spenser's wife now and wondering if they'd ever had children. It seemed sometimes in recent weeks that all he'd ever learn about Geradgery was how much he didn't know. A few hundred people only and yet he felt he'd hardly seen her till this morning. Even his own parishioners had moved outside that closed and total sphere of his own preoccupations. If Barker had cared a little more for the truth he might well have come up with something more telling to justify suspension. Self-absorption perhaps? Of that Benton would gladly acknowledge himself guilty.

'C'mon, David, what do you reckon, anyway?'

'Well, it's doggerel, of course—but it's probably sincere. The argument's clear enough.' Spenser couldn't accept this reserve. He dug around some more and came up with a leaflet.

'What about this, the "Would to Godders"? You ought to know about them anyway. Would to God I was twenty years younger and all that.' Spenser's eyes crinkled a little in anticipation of a joke, even if the long stiffness of Benton's presence was less than conducive. 'Here it is, have a look yourself.' Benton spread the cartoon in front of him and saw a little weasel of a man on a stump haranguing half a dozen listeners, all of whom bore a placard around their necks. *Would to God I were a man!* shouted a termagant. *Would to God I had sons to serve my King and Country!* declared a withered spinster. *Would to God my business responsibilities were lighter!* affirmed a plutocrat with cigar. *Would to God I were physically fit!* said a moribund man at the edge of the group. Benton smiled rather than laughed. Too much of it was familiar: the talk as it used to be outside after morning service; the talk over tea and sandwiches at farewells like Johnny Bartrim's; the talk at the Royal which Benton knew of but had never shared in. And it was so easy to add, 'Would to God I weren't a parson!'

'Not bad, eh? Here Shirl, have a look at this,' said Spenser handing it up to his wife near the stove. 'Well, what about Friday dinnertime then?' he went on, turning to Benton. 'You game? Short notice, I know, but it's only two weeks off, the big day. We'll get some of these posters up and a notice or two scattered about. Get to the cockies before they turn around and go home. I should be able to get a split shift.' Spenser paused, hardly bothering to notice Benton's apprehension. 'Might try to get old Wally Tippet again. He's pretty good value—at that time of the day anyway. What do you think? Ex-digger, priest and a union man. Not a bad trio. Should go well.' He reached for the posters again. 'Stick some of these up in a few windows, on a few lamp posts—church door, what do you reckon?'

Something about the last image got through to Spenser's sense of humour. Benton saw it was probably another perspective on the same set of incongruities he himself already envisaged. Man of God with brush and glue enduring the scorn of shopkeepers or lurking at night to slap sedition up on lamp posts. Friday on the post office steps would hardly be his forte either, less dignified perhaps than those glazed eccentrics down by Central Station with self-abasement as their only weapon. For one who'd condescended gently from the pulpit (and this increasingly was what Benton felt he'd done for five years), it could well be quite an initiation. The Domain speech for Frizelle would not be so bad; the tumult, the crowd, the other speakers would carry the day. Home ground on a cockies' Friday was different altogether.

It wasn't till he was three blocks away and nearing the viaduct that Benton finally understood what the posters he was carrying were really for and the nature of his promise.

Back home, in the kitchen when he got them out, the posters were standard pro-forma: a huge *VOTE NO* and the word *RALLY* almost as tall; then blanks to be filled with where, when and featuring whom. Using some of Billyjim's first box of crayons Amy helped fill them out on the table after dinner; then ran up some flour-and-water paste. By ten Benton, armed with half a billyful and an old paint brush from the pantry, was on his way down to the main street. The shops on either side were as half-lit and deserted as he'd hoped, but to go slapping posters on shopfronts without permission was more than he could readily manage. Nothing in his home or schooling had prepared him for this. He imagined with some resentment the ease, even the relish, with which Spenser would do such a thing.

Veranda poles would serve for a start. McCormick the saddler and the Hibernian could almost be risked, but it was better to ask. As he advanced on the first pole with paste, poster and brush, he felt the same cold point in his stomach he'd felt years before, returning from his one cherry raid on Jenkins' orchard (three bicycles in the moonlight wheeling in at last behind the gym; 'Holy Joe' Benton and the two fifth formers who'd forced him to go). Sergeant Rawson and Constable Hannan would long since have closed the Royal and Hibernian, or at least compelled the transfer of business to the back bar. He had no wish to meet them now. They must know at least as much as everyone else and probably something of Barker and the suspended licence too. Rawson, with those easygoing and omniscient eyes, would not need to say a thing to let him know he'd let down the side and could now, at a stroke, be classed with the park drunks and Aborigines who from time to time had to be thrown into the lockup for their own good. They at least, his eyes would say, didn't know any better.

Steadying amateurishly the first of his posters on its film of wet flour Benton, seeing his own name there, felt again that teetering sensation he'd known just two months back composing his crucial sermon, the same abyss; everything he'd written then had led him to this moment. *Suffer ye thus far ... it is enough.* 'Cockies' Friday', the flat farmers' faces under their brims, the squatters' sons in jodhpurs and sportscoats, a few sales assistants with their twenty minutes off, the farmers' wives, pausing between the baker's and general store, the wives perhaps from his former congregation, come to see what new foolishness was possible. Looking at his name there, exposed, promised, led him on to wonder who might replace him the following Sunday. Barker's dean, he guessed, Denning-Jones, a man of the bishop's own cut, released (it was understood) from cathedral duties to work fulltime with the State Recruitment Committee and now come back preaching universal service, *a prospect most desirable in the sight of God and man.* Benton had seen such a sermon summarised in the *Express*. The dean, as he soon let you know, was a Cambridge man, like Barker himself, and even on the few occasions when he and Benton had seen eye to eye (a synod before the war), the difference was total: Denning-Jones, the breezy metropolitan and Benton, cautious, provincial, articulate under pressure. The sermon would be fluent, that much was certain, if one could bear to go.

In the next half-hour he managed about twenty posters, growing bolder as he worked and almost getting to like the skim of the brush on lifting paint and hardwood. He could feel his notoriety growing up one side of the street and down the other. Spenser, Tippet and Benton; a vaudeville trio almost—(another time, another place ...). It was strange enough anyway. At one point as he was slapping one up on a pole near the post office, a sudden car came surging through, its carbide lamps flaring, as if the whole town were no more than a paddock. Benton was caught against the shopfront, *in flagrante delicto*, frightened but almost laughing too, as the car, without pausing, roared north for Glen Innes.

At last, heading home between street lamps, Benton felt his pulse slow down a little, the adrenalin of his mischief ease. The cosmos, black and moonless above him, looked especially deserted, despite its few thousand visible stars. Briefly he wondered who might really be closer to God. Denning-Jones, perhaps ... but on a night like this it was a distance no-one could cover. If the Kingdom were within that didn't change things much either, another vacuum. Under the dull flare of the last street lamp near the church he checked his watch. Ten forty. A little after midday in the Pozières sector. And somewhere there, a wooden cross with Jack underneath—silenced, scornful.

Benton's dreams that night, when he reached them at last, prefigured the next morning. Teachers from fifteen years ago stood in for local shopkeepers. Buttinger, the maths master, had somehow contrived a grocer's apron and could 'not see my way clear to allowing any poster in my window'; it 'didn't do' to put off customers. And what in any case was Benton of the Lower Sixth, a reliable lad by all accounts, doing tied up with something like this? Benton, muzzled in his dream, could find no answer. Nor could he find one when old Gaffer, the headmaster turned haberdasher, presented the same question. As if on cue a ring of parasolled and hatted ladies demanded of him the same information. As he surfaced from the confusion he realised, though it made little difference, that Gaffer, the haberdasher, was in fact Barker, the bishop. It ought to have made him smile but failed to do so. He lay there beside Amy, staring at the ceiling, letting it float away. There was a high, light drumming of crickets. Spenser had nominated a few shops he'd catch up with after work; the rest were Benton's. In no hurry to rejoin his dreams he thought instead of his mother and a ceiling not much different out at Wallagundah. The crickets came through everywhere like the distant upper frequencies of gunfire.

Though his dreams had left few marks it was with some sense of repetition, as well as nervousness, that he began to bail up the shopkeepers next morning. Cyril Somerton he missed altogether. What was the point, with that soldier/shirker poster already on his door? McCormick, the saddler, proved more than amenable, though he took some time to recover from the shock of actually seeing Benton in his shop. Benton till now had only ever seen the saddler through the refractions of the window. Before starting Benton had stood there a moment looking around the walls: bridles, harness, saddles, stockwhips, a general whiff of linseed and tanning. It seemed a strange contrast with what was now being daily attempted by some of his clients in France. Aub McCormick was a quiet man, forty or so, whom Benton, with a conscious romantic flourish, could imagine as a blacksmith gently beating swords to ploughshares. 'No problem,' said Aub, and his short smile as Benton left was, even with the collaboration of Spenser, the most encouraging sign he'd had from anyone save Amy.

At the Royal he had to track the manager down in the public bar. A large, fat-knuckled man, he looked up from the till at Benton's collar with embarrassment, as if once he'd made some promise to God and the bailiff now had come to foreclose. Benton, in the immanence of stale beer, was equally embarrassed as he got out his request. A poster in the saloon bar?

'Don't know about that,' the man said, looking at what Benton had spread out on the bar. 'Not sure what the gentlemen in there would make of that.'

'How about the door of this one, then?' Benton reshuffled his short list of favours. The Royal's saloon bar, apart from the ladies' lounge upstairs, was, as everyone conceded, the only respectable drinking place in town, a Friday necessity for anyone with more than a few hundred acres. Of all the local landowners it was only those few original families with their private chapels who did not need to grace the Royal saloon, their overseers standing in for them. As Benton thought about all this (and the manager made his break out the back), he noticed three men (shearers? fettlers?) looking bemusedly at him from the far end of the counter; they were lit by a shaft of amber light through a doorway. There was a sign to the saloon bar behind them, a door, it was clear, they'd never pass, regardless of how far their cheques might go in either place. They stared at him without deference or contempt and were still doing so as he left.

The Royal's response—and the mutual embarrassment of both manager and suppliant—proved typical. Even the Hibernian played it safe. Perhaps Bert Spenser, unionist, would have better luck there. So, having finally given up, Benton stopped outside the post office and examined the de facto stage presented by its twin sets of steps and its two granite pillars. He pictured himself in action: no respectful introduction, no hushed hall or nave, just the three of them standing in a row—Spenser, Tippet and Benton, the tall, the short and the one-legged. Which would he rely on? Not Spenser; there was always something oversimple and finally ulterior about him; not Tippet certainly—though the man, with his drunkenness and crutches, exemplified only too well the impact of what all three opposed. Benton himself? A man of God whom God had lost faith in? A man of the cloth—which his bishop had stripped away? A man of conviction—who had turned himself about?

The whole prospect of Friday brought him back something he thought he'd forgotten. Once on a trip to Sydney as a student he'd seen the evangelists near Central Station, and though at that time his faith included the simple dichotomies of theirs he shrank away almost guiltily from the tambourines. The apostles, he knew, had done their share of preaching on corners, but that had been different. Proselytising and Anglicanism did not, he felt, despite the occasional public mission, go comfortably together and for this Benton as an awkward nineteen-year-old student had been just a little grateful. Belief, even its promulgation, was preferably discreet and private. Why should the purities of ritual, the subtleties of thought be sullied in the street? But now, like the tambourine bangers, he'd be there himself, armoured this time not so much with faith as with his secular opinion, an area where he could pretend to no more than his audience. As he surveyed the stage however, it was more with the pre-curtain nerves of an actor than with any shortage of conviction.

Maybe, thought Benton, as he began to walk homewards with his surplus roll of posters, through the alternating light and shade of the verandas (noting, as he passed, his work of the night before), this remoteness, this isolation was a kind of preparation. He thought of John the Baptist and was ashamed. It was not so much a matter of prelude or consequence but of distance. He felt again the averted eyes, the unseeing glances. And again there were just those few who, with a sidelong smile, seemed to whisper their support; workers mostly or their wives (Mrs Spenser, for instance), whom he'd never quite be able to name though they'd been in town at least as long as he had. As a faction, however, they could not exist and there was no hope of their support on Friday. It would not be their minds he'd be trying to change.

In mid-sentence Benton paused and looked out over the pumping of his heart to Bartrim's General Store (where was the counterjumper now?) focusing without thought on a horse outside it, hitched to a veranda post and shifting its weight from one haunch to the other.

'Get back to your pulpit, you skypilot; you're a bloody disgrace, that's what you are.' At just a little past noon the voice was already hard with alcohol.

'Yes, indeed,' said Benton, 'and glad I'd be to do so, especially were I to see you among the congregation, though I suspect the Royal is a more likely venue.' An appreciative ripple ran through the twenty or so who had slowed for a moment's diversion outside the post office and found themselves staying. Benton half wished Amy had been there to hear it.

'No doubt some of you are asking what a man of the cloth is doing on such a platform ... though I must say it seemed harmless enough six months ago on a ... rather more colourful one for the State Recruiting Committee.' Out of his left eye Benton saw Bert Spenser frowning; a couple of his mates from the station out there in the crowd shared the expression. Knowing it was dangerous, this confessional approach, he pressed on anyway. The drunk who'd sparked it off was, as if on Benton's orders, veering off already up the street to the Royal.

'And why am I not saying all this up at St Jude's? Because, ladies and gentlemen, I have been suspended by my bishop for holding the views I offer to you today and am therefore no longer permitted to preach.'

'I should think so, too,' came an audible undertone.

'So far in this war we have had persuasion only, the public and private pressures as it were, and Heaven knows they are powerful enough—but from the 28th, tomorrow fortnight, my friends, there will be no choice. All those eligible will be mustered and sent. Those of you who've tried to get exemptions from Mr Hughes' so-called Home Service call-up will know just what that means. How many indeed are in camp now, awaiting your approval to send them to the guns?'

Among those who formed the core, around the outside of which the others paused and flowed (often with an embarrassed glance, as if at two dogs fornicating in the street), Benton noticed a scattering of weathered, reddish faces under wide brims and the ties, coats and jodhpurs of the smaller landholders. Something had held them. Two months earlier, he knew, they would have scornfully stalked by.

Again Benton paused, looking at them, distracted by how closely the crowd before him matched his foreshadowings. Everything, even the hard noon light, was as if for the second time. Spenser and Tippet (the latter casual on his crutches, as if at any moment he might roll a cigarette) stood to either side of him just as he'd imagined, and the thirty listeners stared at him in the same tight silence, broken only by the sound of horseshoes and cartwheels on the asphalt up the street. There'd not been a single car go by since they'd started. As he looked at them wordlessly, he knew there could not be any who did not know someone who'd opened a door to one of his telegrams; some among them here would still be waiting.

'Let us agree then, ladies and gentlemen, that whatever the original rights and wrongs of August 1914 might have been, the war by now, two bloody and inconclusive years later, must be stopped.'

'Tell that to the Kaiser's mob,' called a new voice on the right.

'Yeah, maybe you've got a direct line, eh rev?' suggested another voice from the same direction. Several angry heads turned—Benton at least had got them that far. And now he saw who they were. There was the car too, sleek and solid, across the street by Elder Smiths.

'And the first thing we can do to stop it,' he went on, ignoring them as he'd done before on this same set of steps, 'is to vote NO on the 28th. The road to the conference table, to peace with honour, a negotiated peace, starts there.' He decided to leave it at that and stepped back a little to the sound of a few hands clapping. Spenser's cronies from the station were the main ones, he noticed.

'A coward's way, if ever there was,' sneered McEwan. Benton was in no doubt this time.

'And why don't you go, young man, you're so brave,' said a farmer's wife with a force which seemed to surprise even herself.

'Don't worry, madam,' the young man said, with a short, caustic bow. 'I will be just as soon as I turn eighteen. There's no doubt of a McEwan's loyalty.'

'And now, ladies and gentlemen,' announced Spenser, cutting in hurriedly with his impresario's tone, 'the man we've all been waiting for, Lance Corporal Wally Tippet, late of the A.I.F. and wounded at Gallipoli, as you can see.'

'C'mon, Ian,' said McEwan to his friend. 'I think we've heard enough without staying to hear a man who'd rat on his mates.' Though Spenser hadn't heard it, Tippet had.

'You young cockies' whelps,' he called after them as they strolled across to the big car with its half-moon silver headlights. 'You wouldn't last a day. You're all talk.' The crowd turned back to Tippet as if mutely to apologise for the youths' poor taste.

'Yes, ladies and gentlemen,' Tippet began, 'unlike most of you, I've been there and ...' It was much the same speech as Benton had heard at the railway institute. Benton, standing there in the sun which had a good deal of heat in it now, wondered what the audience would be making of the slept-in looking uniform Tippet still wore and the single campaign ribbon which seemed only to emphasise the lack of others. The story of his pension of seven and six did not go so well this time, though the frequent references to his mates in Shrapnel Valley or still vertical in France were poignant enough. 'Sterling blokes to a man.' At least in this situation, Benton realised, he as a clergyman had the novelty of having swapped from pulpit to soapbox and Spenser, for his part, had the practised indignation of the long-time union man. But Tippet, as he went on, attracted only pity, a regret that the war had not been decorous enough to keep its distance and had left instead this somewhat unseemly deposit on their very own doorstep.

Spenser perhaps had been thinking along similar lines, for it wasn't long before he broke in with: 'Yes, thank you, Wally. Wally Tippet, ladies and gentlemen, ex-A.I.F., a man who knows what it's really like. When he says how to vote you can be sure he knows what he's talking about. He's seen the gratitude of Billy Hughes and Senator Pearce at first hand—and what their promises mean. Another thing to keep in mind in two weeks' time.' Spenser hesitated, not quite sure of how to wind it up and fill the space his rivals would have filled with 'God Save the King'. 'Well, thanks for your attention, folks, and don't forget to spread the word. Vote NO.'

Under his wave which was almost a clenched fist the remaining fifteen or so onlookers silently moved on. Benton rolled up the calico *VOTE NO* banner which had hung over the railing and gave it to Spenser who was getting set to drive Tippet back to the station for the afternoon train. Having forgotten that Spenser still had a shift to finish, Benton had thought of asking him and his friends back to the rectory for a post-mortem and maybe a cup of tea, but as they all piled up into one of the railway's spring carts and Spenser flicked the horse into motion, he did not regret the way things had turned out.

Hurrying on his way home, and still somehow nervous, Benton, hungry now, was pushed as if by spiritual exercise to consider why he'd not really spoken to Tippet and why he was relieved rather than saddened by the railwaymen's inability to take up his unmade offer. It was not so much that in these last weeks he'd been 'sent to Coventry', as the school phrase had it, but that he'd come to perceive the isolation that had been there all along. He had seen, at a distance, a certain friendship among others even though the town itself, with all its separate, self-reliant lives, did not seem to offer it much scope. Sometimes, finding himself stalled between inquiries at the church door, or walking into the church hall after evensong, he had felt its absence acutely but had told himself it was simply the fate of the family man (though, when he thought about it, it had long preceded Billyjim). It was something in the calling itself. Believers, unbelievers, parishioners, townsmen never quite talked to him as they did among themselves. Benton (any clergyman?) suggested by his very presence shortfalls of resolution they'd rather not recall. When their minister passed on with his innocuous and lofty smile to the next group, they seemed at once to re-enter their normal selves, just as the next group abandoned theirs at his approach. Exceptions were rare. In those earlier days Mrs Giddins, in her rector's presence, seemed to experience a sudden perfection, as though for a moment before his appearance there had existed the possibility of her being less than correct on every score. Cyril Somerton was another, a man with whom Benton might almost have held the extended conversation which often, after a choir practice or a service, seemed about to begin but which usually ended with an abstracted pause on Benton's part and Somerton's abrupt departure. There had at least been mutual respect, each man in the other's eyes doing a journeyman's job.

Whether at church door or in the street, everyone, it seemed to Benton now, had been simply the embodiment of some obligation, some pattern of family circumstance (to be memorised if possible), a giver of that mild and slightly embarrassed respect which somehow served instead of friendship. Even those with a comparable education, old Doctor Evans and Preston, the lawyer who split his practice between

Geradgery and Armidale, were no different really. They too, confronted by that collar and its leanly well-intentioned wearer, would give the same respectful nod and step away from pleasantries.

Twice in these last weeks, walking through that sightless scattering of cockies' Friday shoppers, Benton had had the impulse to rip off his collar—and had known immediately that such an act could only be the beginning of something too complex and lengthy ever to be accomplished.

And yet for all that fraternity among the uncollared, for all that camaraderie at the Hibernian and something more restrained at the Royal, that straining at the leash of young McEwan and his offsider, it was only he, it seemed, who truly sensed what was happening in France. Even for those who'd accepted his telegrams, it was only a personal grief, an aberration to be protested or withstood—but only ever in personal terms. The war was some slow, far distant, natural catastrophe, like floods in India, which inexplicably emptied the beds in their own houses and offered no explanation of itself, let alone the idea of its possible interruption.

In a paradoxical way Benton, helplessly eloquent on the post office steps, had actually felt closer to his audience than he'd ever felt in the closed-off comfort of St Jude's. The resonance of brick and rafter was ultimately indulgent; the voice dispersing in the glare of a midday street was closer, for all its higher volume and political content, to that other, inner voice the audience might hear for themselves in the last grey minutes of the night, uneasy soliloquies silenced by the first roosters or the thud of an axe, by the beginnings of movement on the streets. It was not so much what he'd said as the tone—or the undertone. It was the voice, he hoped, for which the snarls of young McEwan and the drunk had been merely the roosters. Somehow, Benton knew, he would be a kind of channel, a leakage perhaps, between those unremembered murmurs of four a.m. and the

daylight imperatives to follow, the full daylight in which the
war occurred and, being still twelve thousand miles away in
France could never quite be seen to happen.

## 2 4

Amy, waiting in the front room, must have seen him coming across the lawn. She opened the door for him but her gaze seemed focused on something much further off.

'How did it go?'

'Not too bad,' said Benton, looking round vaguely for Billyjim; then remembering the afternoon nap. 'Thirty or so, I guess. It's a start.' Without seeming to have heard she led him into the drawing room and as they sat down on the sofa she handed him a lettergram, military grey. 'Jack' was all she said and, getting up again, moved close to the glass, staring through a single panel into the afternoon, the new leaves of English trees. David took up the irresolute scrawl which, following his own cautious hand at school, had caused some comment and, pausing just a moment, with an inhalation of breath, tore at the perforation.

*7.9.16*

*Dear Davey,*

*It's not really been a grudge you know—though we've had our differences, you might say. You've seen the odd letter I've written to Mum, I suppose, just to keep her courage up (and mine, perhaps) but now with this last couple of days just back from the Pozières business I reckon it's about time you knew a bit about what it's really like— censor permitting, that is!*

*France is a lot different from Gallipoli. Fritz's 9.2s and maxims make sure of that. Even in the first round a month back a third of our battalion was skittled. Now with this show we're almost two-thirds gone, including Frank Dalton. You'd remember him, I think.*

Went right off at the end and charged the whole German line. He was almost at the wire before they got him. Paul Molloy, the sergeant (I don't think you knew him), was knocked too just outside our forward trench when we were falling back from getting too far in front of one of those Tommy New Army divisions. A shell knocked his leg half off and he lay there bleeding for two hours before any of us could get out to drag him in. I don't suppose they put much in those telegrams but it'd be good if you could say something to his mother. He was the only mate I ever really had—and tough. Up near Ben Lomond's his address. God knows how it took the Boche so long to get him. He risked his neck for the rest of us often enough.

The chaplain, Phil Watkins, says he might be up Armidale way when he gets back but that won't be for a few months yet, lucky bugger. 'Fearless Phil', they call him. He's not too bad though. A front line trench is not much of a place at any time, let alone without a .303. He doesn't talk much about it either, just a bit sometimes at the burials down the line.

You know, Davey, when I first got here and saw our men blown to pieces and moaning for bearers and the dead in their trenches and in ours I wanted to rub your prim little Godly nose in it. I thought of one of those sermons you gave just before I joined up. The cause may be just, even holy as you say, but the methods certainly aren't. After this last show what's left of us aren't too sure about anything except maybe our mates. They don't tell us any figures, of course, but you can see them just the same. Just multiply who's gone from your company roll across the whole division and you get the picture quick enough. The war's not over yet, you can tell them that, if you like. They say now that the 'Little Digger' is going to hold a vote on whether people ought to be forced to fight or not. We could certainly do with some help, that's for sure, but I'm not too sure about conscription. It's bad enough when you've volunteered. Guess you'll be stirring for a YES vote though. They reckon there's an ex-padre over in D company now tore off his collar and joined up in the first week. Quite a character too, by all accounts.

Some of the fellows say if you've been through Pozières you'll come through anything. Could be—but whatever way it turns out I want *you to know I've had all three of you in mind, not just Mum, but you and Lyall too. That time with all five of us there at Wallagundah not long before Dad died, you remember. It's a kind of lucky charm memory, that one, though I didn't realise it at the time. Better than the later times with you up there in your pulpit and Lyall being so bloody quiet and cocksure. That earlier time is what I take with me and not much else. You don't hear much of that God, King and Country stuff out here but you hang on just the same—and the other blokes hang on for you. What would you call that? 'Greater love ...'?*

*Give my love to Mum but don't show her this. There's no point in her knowing it's any worse than she imagines.*

*Yours ever,*
*Jack*

Benton put it down and looked up at Amy, still standing against the front window. He took it up again, feeling the light cardboard in his fingers, imagining its six week journey. He looked at the date: three days before the tenth. They must have been sent straight back up the line. He could see the letter, sealed with Jack's tongue, in a military bag to Paris, London, on a troopship at Southampton (with its ballast of disabled), then the four or five weeks on the intervening oceans, looping its way at last round the southern cities, then northwards interminably on the Glen Innes Mail. The telegram starting its journey four days later had flashed through that long umbilical to be decoded first in Melbourne, split up into hundreds more (each with the Minister's *PROFOUND SYMPATHY AND DEEP REGRET*), then decoded finally by that telegraphist whom Benton had never seen or spoken to but whom he nevertheless felt he knew quite well. It was an invisible conspiracy to whom young Frank, the delivery boy, was also a party. Amy, at the window, must have felt David's lifted gaze on her back for she turned at last and came over. Benton held the lettergram up to her. She sat down beside him and began to read.

Actually, as Amy remembered a few minutes after she finished Jack's, there'd been another letter too, forgotten in the shock of that name, rank and number. It was from Denning-Jones, the dean, and regretted to inform Benton that following the bishop's (*His Lordship's*) decision to withdraw Benton's licence to officiate, he, Denning-Jones, would be celebrating next Sunday's communion. He did rather hope in view of Benton's knowledge of church law, and the unfortunate background to the present impasse, that there would be no acrimony on either side and that a seemly and Christian service might be held.

The only surprise in the whole letter was the omission of the word 'patriotic'. Barker most certainly could not have resisted, but for Denning-Jones seemliness was next to Godliness and there was no point, clearly, in needless offence. That at least was one difference between protégé and mentor.

## 25

Unable to explain it, even to himself, Benton, the following Sunday, was crossing the gravel to St Jude's, 'Now Thank We All Our God' filtering firmly through stained glass and brick. Still wearing his collar and stock, he was almost immobilised by the sheer normality of it all. Apart from his position outside the door rather than up by the altar nothing might ever have happened.

> *Who from our mother's arms*
> *Hath blessed us on our way ...*

These voices were not the scattered, self-conscious few who had stuck to him throughout. The choir with Somerton back at the helm was in full sail again, and even from outside he thought he could hear Mrs Giddins' soprano billowing in relief (and pride perhaps, for wasn't this the dean himself?) out and away over the rest.

Not taking a prayer book, Benton slipped in the main door and stood alone in the back pew. A few heads turned, half-smiled and were averted quickly.

> *And guide us when perplexed*
> *And free us from all ills*
> *In this world and the next.*

Benton did not feel like joining in. Some might have said he was sulking but it was more the realisation of how much separated him from his congregation (or 'flock', as Denning-Jones would have it). Their relief was so tangible it could almost be felt between the fingers. What had they done, after all, in far Geradgery to deserve such unseemliness, such perversity?

Watching the dean at work now, the well-cleansed skin, the slightly long but well-groomed hair, Benton could not but admire his style. The prosperous childhood, the elocutionary training, the unquestioned faith in the Trinity and in each of the thirty-nine separate articles combined to give him that assurance, that metropolitan whiff, in which the parishioners of Geradgery, various as they were, could find such satisfaction. A little too much would bring suspicion but the dean, it seemed, knew just where to stop.

He passed on into the commandments. *'God spake these words and said: I am the Lord, Thy God. Thou shalt have none other Gods but me.'* As the congregation sought God's help to incline their hearts to keep this law, Benton thought again of Marcion's creator-judge and couldn't help wondering what other demiurges crowded their hearts: a good day's work for a good day's pay, clean shoes, pressed suits, and a righteous anger (akin to God's, no doubt) at the wilful trespass of the German race. On the contents of Mrs Giddins' heart (as she sat up the front beneath her proud white hat and its clutch of feathers) Benton did not care to think.

As the sixth commandment came and went, Benton added mutely, 'Unless of course in a noble cause' and wondered if anyone else there might be adding the same proviso. The Lord inclined their hearts and those of their sons in France to keep this one also. The adultery prohibition got about the same attention as that on murder. Something of the kind might occasionally be seen on the other side of the viaduct, but short of an appreciative glance at Mrs Thurmond's daughter, titian-haired and suddenly well-dressed (from a small inheritance, Amy had heard), or at young Ted Franklin's wife, fresh from a Sydney finishing school, adultery with its filigree of lies was altogether too foolish. Benton certainly had no designs on any wife there and had never noticed any such impulse directed at

Amy either, even though she was, Benton had long suspected, more sensual than most.

As Denning-Jones breezed through to the creed, Benton was even more divided. '*I believe in one God, the Father Almighty, Maker of Heaven and earth, and of all things visible and invisible.*' The inexorable forward movement of the theology (creation, incarnation, suffering, redemption, judgement) made a kind of seamless metaphor which did not permit escape or demur at any point. It carried you through. For fifteen years it had carried Benton with it. '*And I look for the resurrection of the dead, and the life of the world to come. Amen.*'

And yet were there not now other metaphors coming to replace it, uglier images, not all of them in photographs, some from nightmares, others from the future—the square miles of white crosses, the memoirs of generals, the obituaries of statesmen, and how many thousands dead on the Somme? *And I look for the resurrection of the dead.* (Jack?) As he mouthed the words, Benton felt their meaning swerve away from him and saw instead Jack's mate, Frank Dalton, running crazily in no-man's-land and the tight-lipped Paul Molloy awaiting rescue. As Jack had said in his letter, David too wished to shove such images, like roadside carrion, under their relieved and proper noses, under this interloper's delicate nostrils. With all that pomade up at the altar, and a whole twelve thousand miles to waft, the smell from France dispersed a little. Even in London apparently it was pretty mild—and yet the sounds which had taken them as volunteers to Flanders and the Somme (*The bugles of England calling o'er the sea*) had been vivid enough—still were if young McEwan and his friend were any guide. So too in a way were those telegrams which swung down round the world. *IT IS WITH DEEP REGRET.*

Denning-Jones was up in the pulpit now and while the tensions provoked by the creed continued for Benton, the dean's words, their general drift, came to him fragmented, simplified, as if in primitive translation. There must have been something there about this not being a moment for division or recrimination, whether in church or nation. Nor, the dean must have insisted, was it a time for extremism, unless perhaps in His Majesty's cause and then only if tempered by the Christian spirit. What surely was more important, the dean would have thought, was the totality of the Master's message and not the distortion of it which might be made by wrenching one small part or another out of its context.

There had been, the dean suggested, some unfortunate confusion in these matters recently among the people but they must ensure now that good sense prevailed. Certainly there was the great issue to be considered in less than a fortnight, the critical issue of the government's plans to reinforce our courageous young men at the Front. This was, however, something on which all must search their own conscience, though he for one had no doubts that a negative vote would be a great boon to the Germans—he would say no more than that for the present. The Lord said, 'Love your neighbours as yourself,' and that was the spirit he would commend to them in the coming weeks. 'And now to God the Father, Son and Holy Ghost ... Let us pray for the whole state of Christ's church militant here on earth.'

At the communion rail now from which Benton held back there were perhaps three score in all, crowding on their knees in turn for the bread and wine, the body and blood, of which they, or most of them, had these last three months been so unreasonably deprived. '*Ye that do truly and earnestly repent you of your sins and are in love and charity with your neighbours draw near with faith ...*'

Benton, so dearly wanting that wider peace elsewhere, would gladly have made this lesser one with Denning-Jones and gone forward, for, after all, the priest, he knew, was an instrument only—but he could not. As much as his desire not to compromise all he'd so far said and done, it was those first few words of the call to confession which prevented him. *Ye that do truly and earnestly repent* ... He had his sins surely enough, but not perhaps the ones this gathering was keen to load on him. No, not the sins of treachery, ingratitude, cowardice perhaps, but rather those less obvious sins—isolation, incomprehension, self-satisfaction—all significant enough but dwarfed nevertheless by the juggernaut he was confronting. Concern for his own petty catalogue was near to self-indulgence. They were things to be worked out, with or without God's grace. Watching the communicants come back down the aisle, Benton wondered what greater or lesser sins they in their turn might not quite have repented. It was chastening how even though God Himself appeared to have withdrawn beyond the rim of His creation, the long legacy of sin and Christ's surmounting of it were still there.

Thus, finally, as the sustained, uneasy metaphors of 'Onward Christian Soldiers' rang out from Somerton's departing choir, there was nothing to make Benton change his mind. He tried to slip away quickly but Denning-Jones, not much slower on his feet than Barker, it seemed, had deftly managed to be at the door first to shake hands. Benton, one of the first out, saw no point in refusing. Their eyes met and held for several seconds. The dean did rather seem to regret this business, but Mrs Giddins with her white hat and strong forearms saved him nicely by almost elbowing Benton aside and saying: 'I did so much appreciate your sermon, dean, so uplifting in our time of need. You will of course be ...' The voice faded as Benton re-crossed the gravel to the vicarage, deserting, he knew, the few who'd stuck by him but needing even more the only reassurance that he knew these days, the support which had shrunk to the twelve squares of a single house and was embodied in Amy and Billyjim, those other two flanks to his resistance. With Billyjim clamouring in his arms at the front door, Benton glanced back over his shoulder and noticed for the first time what must have been the bishop's car, the mudguards, headlights and bonnet of which projected beyond the far side of the church. An impression of its solidity, polish and readiness for forward movement lingered on his eye as he made his way to Amy down the hall.

**26**

Though Denning-Jones could only be spared on Sundays his luminous, orthodox presence there in the pulpit neatly finalised Benton's removal. Once more on Wednesday Somerton could be heard rehearsing his choir. Once more Mrs Giddins was attending to flowers in the church and tea in the hall. The tennis club, however, did not revive so easily. Too many of its best young men were down in Armidale already in camp awaiting the all clear on Saturday week. Those who had managed their exemptions were mainly graziers' sons who played their tennis elsewhere.

It was all rather like a town band, Benton fancied, which, having fallen out with its conductor, winds up its affairs only to regroup the next week with all its members but one. Benton was still uncertain about just what the withdrawal of a licence meant. Services obviously, but visits? Religious Instruction?

As the week drew on towards the Domain it was all an increasingly pointless question. With his own faith failing, or so sea-changed, he was hardly in a position to shore up anyone else's. There was no market for doubt—Denning-Jones had shown that. Benton could still see Mrs Giddins' face from last Sunday, radiant with resumption, as if plucked from drowning. Somerton's eyes through his rimless glasses had a vaguer version of the same expression, Benton's few silent and sidelong supporters on the street were not to be seen in St Jude's anyway, though they did remind him that his doubt was something positive too. From the *Herald* he still got from Somerton's every day, he could tell his conviction was no less important even if the worst of Pozières seemed to be over for the moment. You could almost swear Haig was holding off on his final push for the year in deference to the Australian voter. With spring in New England, the first flowers, it seemed an aberration to consider the war. The whole week had been a spacious succession of days, no petal-scattering aftermaths of winter. On such days, out walking, it was possible for Benton to forget for minutes at a time everything which had carried him so far.

Not everyone lost track, however. On Tuesday there was another Manila envelope in the mail with a single sheet of paper saying *GOD SAYS GO* and a single white feather to go with it. On Wednesday night as the descants from the choir were quietly soaring, a few drunks threw some further handfuls of gravel on the vicarage roof before capering away up the street laughing and calling, 'Three cheers for Kaiser Bill, me boys, the parson's only friend.' Or that was how Benton caught it fading away down the street. This time it was not so much that throaty, physical contempt he'd felt in young McEwan's voice but just a piece of mischief unable to pass up its chance. And once, too, in the main street a woman in black of sixty or so had mutely shaken a parasol in his face as if not trusting herself to words.

On the Wednesday late in the afternoon Benton walked across to Spenser's to see what else was being planned. Spenser at his kitchen table seemed as listless as his failing cottage. Last Friday's minor stir, it seemed, had exhausted his initiative. The papers, he admitted to Benton, spoke of huge and fiery meetings in Sydney and Melbourne but here in Geradgery, as they both knew, people did not change their votes in generations, let alone in lifetimes. Faction and party might turn themselves about, but the vote in its essentials stayed the same. Sitting over a cup of tea with Spenser's wife hovering, neither of them said much, but the leaden knowledge of that immutability was all, finally, that Benton had to take with him as he set off home to start his speech for Saturday. Frizelle's confirmation had come by telegram on Tuesday afternoon but it was not till Thursday morning that Benton was able to shake off Spenser's languor and regain a little of what had precipitated that first

sermon—so much, as the bishop had said, against the tenets
of both church and common sense, a distinction in any case
which Barker rarely found it necessary to make.

The shadows of the speech had flickered in his mind all
week but now on Thursday morning with the train to Sydney
only a day away, he finally began. *Ladies and gentlemen, fellow
Australians, I speak to you today as both a clergyman and as a citizen.
Indeed, as the chairman has already said, a clergyman suspended
for the beliefs he holds as a citizen.* At his desk in the drawing
room, he could hear Billyjim out the back somewhere banging
something metallic. *Never has God been so misrepresented as He has
been throughout this war and in the last few weeks of this campaign.*
That would be the line. It was as a clergyman, not as newsagent
or haberdasher, that they'd invited him after all. The absurdity
of *Gott Mit Uns*, that was the starting point. Then on from there
to the Garden of Gethsemane and the sheathed sword, then
back to the Sermon on the Mount. *Render unto Caesar the things
which are Caesar's.* Dangerous perhaps, vague too; though, God
knew, Caesar had had tribute enough in the present conflict,
with Benton's own Anglicans among the most fulsome. The
image returned to him of the crowd, the windblown surface of
hats, the scattered plumes, the harbour beyond the shadows of
fig trees and the sea itself a few miles further off somewhere
beyond that. He too on the edge of such crowds had shared the
general disdain which greets and sticks to anyone who would
mount a soapbox and change the world. Christ had known as
much of this as anyone. The mockery was timeless, as was the
crown of thorns. The accents of that Jerusalem crowd must
surely have been Australian as must the pleading for Barabbas.

## 27

*Sunshine on Saturday brought out billows of white muslin in a foam of frills and tucks and Niagaras of lace falling over the delicate beauty of gossamer drapery. Steam laundries won't be allowed to get their teeth into this summer's best pettis.*

The train was sloping down the long cutting already. Benton, flipping through last week's *Bulletin* in the failing light, had hovered at 'A Woman's Letter', a column which Amy often read but never without ambivalence. Remote and straitened as she was, the frothy milliner's detail and the caustic, knowing tone still offered her something that doctrine and good sense could never quite extinguish. Benton delighted in the sudden gusts of laughter which would escape her at some impossible excess of frivolity or pretension. 'Did you see this?' she'd say and read him something like: *In silky black Mrs Tom Robin made a picturesque relief to the cloud of pink and blue butterflies on the lawn.* To Benton in the last few weeks, however, these posturings on members' enclosures and the governor's lawn, these natty resumés of names, had a touch of the obscene about them. The postures of the dead elsewhere were rather less engaging. Two charitable afternoons per week at the Red Cross knitting drive hardly gave them the right to such frivolity. The train rattled into the valley towards Armidale, cathedral city, where doubtless right now Barker and Miss Pym would be finalising correspondence in that study from which Benton had so abruptly issued scarcely more than a month ago.

*Sydney,* continued 'A Woman', under lamplight now and descending the Moonbis, *still palpitates with the tense patriotism of the women's meeting at the Town Hall. You should have seen our Billy boil over in seething scorn of the agitators who fill housemaids'*

*heads with silly tales of a coming rush of Chinese domestics. A dozen*
*'anti' women, cunningly distributed in the galleries and in the dense*
*mass of the hall, contrived to occasionally keep 4,000 others from*
*hearing the Prime Minister's words. An old dame with a screech like*
*a harbour siren held up the meeting for about ten minutes. Shaking*
*her first from a gallery she was so wedged in with the crowd that it*
*took time to put the muffler of authority over her infuriated hat. In*
*the middle of the hall a touzled female shrieked her defiance of law*
*and order but there were 4,000 other women ready to seize the little*
*man and chair him through the hall. Hankies fluttered in a snowfall*
*of 'Yes'.*

Harridans, viragoes, termagants ... and while the little man
himself was speaking! Had they no sense of decency? Benton
thought fondly of Amy. Given a little more provocation than
she was normally prey to, she too might be a *touzled female*—
and a powerful one at that. 'A Woman' no doubt had intended
belittlement, but the spectacle of the little man himself being
tossed up and chaired on the beldames' shoulders was no less
amusing.

Persistently, as the train, station by station, filled up and shuttled
its way southwards through Werris Creek, Muswellbrook and
Scone, the *touzled female* and the *old dame* returned to Benton's
fleeting half-world of trees, paddocks, rockface and moonlight.
Both, Benton guessed, had opened doors to men like himself,
wrong-footed and stooped with telegrams. *IT IS WITH DEEP*
*REGRET.* He shared with them the hours of staring at a ceiling,
indelible images of a single death. Down the hall maybe was
a last son or brother, seventeen, drawn on and driven back by
turn, trying to walk the streets unbowed, four thousand other
women facing him down ('where's your uniform, young man?
Aren't you ashamed?'), women whose notable reserves of virtue
Jack had died to protect, or so perhaps Barker would be saying
on Sunday.

As the light came up on Hawkesbury sandstone the two
meetings had somehow fused in Benton's brain, four thousand

and twelve women at the town hall in those sandstone galleries, the swirling open thousands in the Domain. Opposite ends of a spectrum but the ferocity was the same. Pozières had made sure of that.

**28**

Frizelle, at Central Station six years on from college, was quite a shock. Benton, split between his cold, sluiced face and the all-night staleness of his body, had stepped down and started walking with the crowd towards the exit. Maybe Frizelle was waiting out there. As he looked out over shifting heads there were fewer slouch hats than he'd expected. He was surrounded by mothers looking for porters and reining in their children. Then someone was tugging at his arm.

'David.'

He looked down. The face from St John's had contracted somehow, dried out. There was a premature fleck of grey in the gingerish hair and an unsuccessful moustache. He might almost have stepped from a recruitment poster—the *weedy shirker*. All he needed was a strongarm mother and pince-nez glasses.

'Jeremy.' Frizzle, the nickname, rose unsummoned to the mind.

'Glad you could make it,' said Frizelle. 'Here, let me take that,' he continued, seizing Benton's valise. 'Got to save your strength, you know.' Benton hung onto it a moment but, seeing how much Frizelle wanted the role, relinquished his bag and walked with him towards the barrier. Frizelle seemed to almost scamper on ahead of him as if clearing the way, asking as he went about the trip down and assuring his guest how pleased everyone was that he'd been able to accept the offer. 'After all,' he said, nearly bumping into a trolley, 'it's not every day we can get an Anglican up on the platform, stood down or otherwise.' He giggled a little. Benton made an awkward smile. Though he'd never actually seen Frizelle in a clerical collar (at St John's that had always been the destination), he still felt offended somehow by its absence. He noted, as Frizelle glanced back towards him, the shiny, tightly knotted tie in its stead and remembered that clean, intense face in the dining room. Something seemed to have gone out of the man. Benton saw him swinging those Indian clubs in the gym—he wouldn't be doing much of that now.

They queued to file through a gate. 'You're not any shorter, then, eh?' said Frizelle as they came through. 'Though our good friend Barker did his best, I suppose.' Again Benton smiled, recalling the earlier Frizelle's humourlessness on the tennis court. It was a strange way he had of joking now: the grey eyes paid his own jokes no attention but bored on steadily into the future.

'What about this morning?' asked Benton as they stood in the great grey echoes of the concourse.

'Let's start with breakfast,' said Frizelle, nipping off briskly with Benton's valise through the crowd.

Even the cigarette annoyed Benton, the way he swept it about unnecessarily and held it ember inwards to the palm. He drank the last of his coffee. It had an aftertaste of chicory, Worcestershire almost, he thought, looking at the cage of condiments on the table.

'Yes,' Frizelle continued, more expansively now, over a sudden clatter of plates. 'It's all been going pretty well. Three thousand they said at the Domain last week. *Herald* said only eight hundred, naturally enough. Some of us from the Peace Society weren't too keen at first. It can get a bit violent sometimes. The police aren't much use either, especially if there are a few soldiers about.' He stubbed his cigarette in the ashtray, slowly and thoroughly as if he'd not long learned to do it. 'No way we could book a hall, of course.'

Benton, staring blankly out a tall window towards the city, had been only half listening. He was more interested now in

why Frizelle was wearing that shiny blue tie—and how he'd
fared down here with the recruiting officers, or the patriotic
women. 'Chest 33'—that might be a problem—or a solution.
His address, Benton remembered, was out on the Bondi line;
he could imagine him swaying on a tram towards it with his
thin-brimmed homburg, his newspaper and his tight, thin tie, a
woman in black fixing him with her eye. *GET INTO KHAKI.* His
students too—what did they think? The curiosity was almost
enough to make him ask.

'What about you, then?' said Frizelle suddenly, as if dodging
Benton's thoughts. 'You think His Lordship is likely to back
down? I suppose with Annie and the child you're in a bit of
a spot.' He seemed to flirt with the irony on 'His Lordship'.
Benton wondered where he'd got the 'Annie and the child'—
he couldn't remember mentioning Amy or Billyjim in letters.
'Course I could try to get you in somewhere at school. There's a
place coming up at the end of the year as it happens.' Frizelle,
Benton saw, was embarrassed now. He'd meant to stop himself
running on—and there he was again.

'Thanks,' said Benton, 'but at this point it's hard to say.' He
smiled, more to himself than to Frizelle. 'Not the best kind of
reference, I suppose, being sacked by a bishop.'

'No,' said Frizelle quickly and without smiling, 'but I could ...'

'Don't worry,' said Benton. 'He hasn't asked the Council to
cut off the money yet. And I have got family in the district.'
As he said it, he could feel the gelding solidly beneath him
on the long spur to the homestead, and smell the sweat as he
unsaddled. He thought of his mother in the kitchen there,
drying the plates after breakfast, and Lyall already out in the
paddocks. And what does God think, Davey?'

Frizelle with two stained fingers was fidgeting with his
tobacco pouch.

'Why did you—?' Benton began suddenly. Why did you get
out? '—think of me for this afternoon? There must be a lot of
union men more experienced.'

'They'll be there, don't worry,' said Frizelle. 'It's just that some of us from the Peace Society wanted to bring in the moral side a bit more. With the unionists there's more talk of Chinese these days than there was in the gold rush. And Maltese, of course.'

'Even go, anyway,' Benton smiled.

'And a Catholic wouldn't have done. The Irish business is something else again. You can't go past the good archbishop down in Melbourne on that.' Frizelle was warming to it now, three butts in the ashtray. There were other reasons too, it seemed, and not a little conflict in the League itself. Some were ready, they insisted, to enlist voluntarily at the end of the campaign just to make their point; others wanted the troops home straight away, whatever happened. Benton, as he listened without following the finer detail, marvelled at the way all Frizelle's energies seemed focused on this one issue of conscription; everything else about him was blurred at the edges, even to the way he dressed and smoked. The nervousness which in most contexts would be irritating or pointless was in Frizelle's case almost a kind of sustenance. Benton's question of why he'd slipped the collar would have to go unanswered. Thinking of Barker and his letter, of Amy and Billyjim, of those cold New England nights and their stellar spaces, of the daylight distances on Geradgery streets and the many wasted hours of staring at an unseen ceiling or gazing vaguely from his drawing room window, Benton knew it was a question for himself now rather than Frizelle—who suddenly in mid-flight saw, with a slight sense of injury, that Benton had long since ceased to listen.

'Well,' he announced, pushing back his chair and reaching for the bill, 'we might as well get on up there to the office. There's always some last-minute hitch.'

By ten that night Benton was in bed in the spare room at Langlee Avenue, where Frizelle still lived with his mother—the address Philip Watkins, the chaplain, had remembered in France. He

stretched, head and toe, against the metal either end, then jacked
his knees up under the blankets. The bed dipped seriously in
the middle. In the bathroom through the wall Mrs Frizelle had
just turned off the taps and Benton imagined her letting herself
down stiffly and lying there at rest in the perfumed water,
gazing along the pale wastage of her body. Benton, some little
time earlier, had lain in the same bathtub and let it soak away
the day a little.

The Domain rally—as Frizelle and the Peace Society lady
had decided afterwards in a Pitt Street café had, all things
considered, gone well. 'Mrs Anna Haywood ...' Benton
remembered Frizelle's hasty introduction by the wagonette,
just as the chairman was about to get things started. '... the
Reverend David Benton.' It had been a firm, direct handshake.
Neither she nor Frizelle, as it turned out, was on the order of
business but right through the meeting, as Benton saw from
his high seat, she worked her way tirelessly through the crowd
handing out leaflets. She had a large, rather confident, maroon
hat which he could see easily from up on the wagonette,
surfacing and sinking in a sea of hats and heads. There'd been
five chairs up there altogether and a lectern. Benton had been
third to speak, sandwiched between two unionist s. 'Mr David
Benton, from Geradgery, up Armidale way, a minister of the
Church of England and suspended by his bishop, it turns out,
for supporting this campaign and opposing the war.'

It had been a cloudless spring day (Benton's own inner
forecast) with a strengthening breeze up from the harbour
over the gardens. His words seemed to radiate and vanish into
it; the fig trees in front and the buildings on Macquarie Street
too distant for rebound. As his voice had mounted in volume
so too had the intensity of his emotion. The speech itself was
much the same as that heard by those thirty midday citizens of
Geradgery Shire, but this time the skin on the back of his head
seemed to stiffen with conviction. 'Vote NO to conscription and
YES to peace with honour, a negotiated peace.' His phrases this

time, though much the same as before, had a new recklessness of tone. Some of the other speakers had not agreed with him. The war with the Kaiser, they thought, should be fought to the finish, but only ever by volunteers. To bring in conscription was merely to give way to the very thing you were fighting.

As the darkness following the tugged light-switch eased, Benton saw again the irregular patterning of windblown hats, the faces lifted towards and then away from the western sun; he felt again the stiff salt edge to the wind and that vaguer awareness of white sails and blue surfaces, the policemen breaking up the fights that swirled on the edges of the crowd, and was glad again of the absence of khaki.

'I've waited seven years to hear that,' Mrs Haywood had said, pressing in on him as he got down off the wagonette afterwards. 'When I think of all those circulars to the clergy about Peace Sunday ...' Frizelle, who'd been out with the leaflets too, was equally pleased, his tight face easing with the sense of a risk taken and a payoff gained. His stocks in the movement, Benton guessed, would notably have risen and with it again his determination.

Now in a room across the hall Frizelle would still be flicking details through his mind and blocking in, perhaps, his after-school schedule for the final week. He'd not been too keen to finish up the talk at supper but Mrs Frizelle had insisted. 'Now, Jeremy, you let Mr Benton get off to bed now; you haven't had your bones jangled all night on a train. I'm sure it was all very successful—let us leave it at that.' And Frizelle, abstracted, obedient, had wheeled the supper things away up the hall to the kitchen.

Mrs Frizelle was out now; he could hear the water spinning down the hole. Benton thought of her wrapped in a big white towel, drying her toes on the white-painted stool and wiping the mist off the mirror to gaze at her face. He wriggled over onto his side, a long question mark with no dot, and tried to settle himself among the random undulations of the mattress. There would be no insomnia tonight, even in this bed. He thought, half-focused, of Amy and Billyjim and worried himself a little about the Saturday drunks from the Royal. 'Three cheers for Kaiser Bill, me boys, the parson's only friend.' He pictured Frizelle in his straight bed across the hall and reached away vaguely for tomorrow night when his body would again find a more generous curve from Amy's shoulders to her toes, her buttocks pushed up firmly against his own lean belly. As he fell away sideways into sleep he could feel already her warmth through his pyjamas.

# PART THREE

PART THREE

*The attitude of most young men*, declared Captain Winters in an impatient longhand, *is one of callous indifference. They simply do not care who wins the war and some say they would be as well off under the German flag as under the Union Jack. Others admit they are too afraid, and seem to take it as a joke that they can own to being cowards.* He looked out the first floor window over the corrugated-iron veranda to the store across the street. The light from lamps and moon together was just enough to pick out the words *J. & B. McIlwraith, General Merchants.* He checked his wristwatch. Eleven thirty. Almost no sound came up from the street, just some mongrel's yap a few blocks away and a car gaining speed towards the edge of hearing. Winters' own car, or rather the committee's (a Packard, graciously lent by the Upton-Smiths), waited downstairs in the stable, its class and dependability being one of the few remaining satisfactions of his whole assignment.

*Tenterfield is absolutely the worst town I have visited from the recruiting point of view. It needs to be awakened to its responsibilities.* Downright infuriating would have been more accurate. One week to go and they knew nothing. It was perhaps the fifteenth town in a row with audiences of several score yielding one or two recruits. Did they all want to wait for the 28th and someone else to make up their minds for them? Women and the older men turned up in droves; the eligibles were studiously absent.

*We were to speak after just one reel of film but the owner, a Mr Taylor, talking of complaints that his picture shows were being turned into recruiting rallies, would not permit us on stage till the show ended at ten thirty p.m. As we took the stage and people saw us in uniform, they immediately began to leave the hall. We did secure a hearing, but got only one recruit.* Winters could still feel the man Taylor's hypocrisy as he offered his commiserations on the empty hall. While Sergeant Dalby had taken the details of their single catch, Winters had been embarrassed for both of them. This the measure of a nation's gratitude? A man who serves at Gallipoli and is wounded for his trouble is left alone with a single recruit? A rickety melodrama holds them for an hour and a half; the peril of their own country can hardly detain them fifteen minutes.

Not that the speeches had been below par either. Dalby, whom Winters could hear now washing his face in the next room, had taken his usual line—unpretentious, down to earth, a man just out to help his mates. Winters, as usual, had pitched things rather higher—the fight for liberty, truth and justice, Australia's freedom and the Hun's defeat. Though Winters' personal belief in such currency was unshaken he could feel nevertheless its long two years' devaluation. Even in *The Recruiter's Handbook* there on the table it said: *The prospect that the Allies would sweep the enemy aside in a vast wave of enthusiasm disappeared and instead of the best the worst has to be faced.*

Not particularly wishing to face it, Winters' mind felt its way back to better days eighteen months before, when the Cooee marchers had footed it from Gilgandra, when he'd refereed those football matches—'Australia' v. 'Germany'—where those 'injured' on the field were replaced by 'recruits' from the crowd. He remembered too the strings of horses (saddled but riderless) led through country towns on which the recruit was invited to swing up, and the tin-can parades with cars done out as H.M.A.S. *Sydney* or artillery pieces. The Union Jack, full-scale or in the top left corner, had been everywhere then, its red and blue primaries matched by city bands on call at a half-day's notice.

*In all these towns,* Winters continued, envisaging with irritation the 'desk man' who would read it, *there is an absence of reject badges and in some cases men are ashamed to wear them.*

*We have also had more trouble in gaining support from prominent citizens and local talent.* He recalled with distaste, even despair, that increasingly frequent evasiveness of eye foreshadowing 'prior engagements' or 'the impossibility of giving assistance at this time'. Even the ministers, let alone the priests, were not as forthcoming as they'd once been, though most were still prepared to advertise a rally from the pulpit or occasionally grace the platform for a prayer before the singing of the National Anthem. Certainly, Winters would (with chagrin) have to admit, they'd had their impact on his style. How had he wound it up tonight? *In the spirit of Christianity, in the cause of civilisation, of liberty and humanity, in the name of mankind and the sight of God now and forever we must win the war.*

He looked again through the lacy, irritatingly feminine, curtains. *General Merchants.* He thought of the tasteless way the shops had all cashed in on it. *EXTRAORDINARY WAR NEWS. Goods will be FIRED out every week till HOSTILITIES cease.* Though the law, after all, his own profession, was hardly exempt either, he supposed. The business of the courts continued. It was all so distant now from that other time on the veldt, from that honed sense of danger on those curiously different African mornings. He could still, if he concentrated, feel the horse underneath him and the dry landscape heightened by gunfire. The weekend soldiery since (with his legal partners' loyal indulgence) had been a definite falling away. Even the shortage of trained officers in 1914 had not won him, as a forty year old, a passage to the front. There'd been that long year's paperwork and, finally, this vital fulltime assignment with the Recruiting Committee—which now in recent weeks had quite lost its edge.

There was something galling in the self-satisfied stupor of these country towns. They had not even the excuse of Irish fecklessness or the bloody-minded self-interest of the city slums, people too ignorant, Winters knew, to be aware of what the Empire brought them every day. The good citizens of Tenterfield however, whose very livelihood depended on those red-shaded dominions all over the globe, had even less appreciation. And now they had the hide to complain of the call-up for local service, this least of preliminaries! It was the same all over. Almost fifty per cent seeking exemption—trouble with shearing, problems with the harvest—even mayors and shopkeepers mouthed the same phrases, one eye as always on votes or the till.

It was close to midnight now. A man needed more sleep than this to be efficient. The report, even as it stood, was too generous by far. What did they know, anyway, down there in the office? There was no sound from the street now, no sound from Dalby either next-door. Winters, at a dead-end, reached for the *Handbook. Advice to Organisers: 10. Avoid all offensive reference of a personal tone. 14. Never lose your temper* (not so easy when you were sickened daily by the shamelessness of those who joke about their own and others' cowardice). *Answers to Objections ... Hints to Organisers ... Pensions: £3 per fortnight maximum rates; loss of one eye—half maximum rate ...* and so on through the permutations to *loss of one eye together with loss of leg, foot, hand or arm—the maximum rate.* Winters allowed himself for a moment to conceive of such a person—a badly lopped tree. He wondered how skilled he might get with his crutches and what his wife might make of him in bed.

It had been damned unfortunate about that Tippet fellow down in Armidale, a positive barrier to recruiting apparently and with only a leg gone after all. Seven and six a week did seem a bit lean when you considered it. Better to be in recruiting, he knew, than in repatriation—they always looked better going onto the ships than coming off. Good old Dalby had the right kind of wound, a slight, almost distinguishing limp; a sliver of steel in the knee—and no pain to speak of (or at least he never spoke of it).

Winters put the booklet down with self-conscious exhaustion—a long day spent in a good cause—and briskly (almost spitefully) cleaned his teeth, checked his revolver in its

holster by the bedside table (needlessly perhaps but it didn't
do to be casual with an Enfield .476, not when you thought of
its reassuring largeness in the palm and its well-known power
to stop a dervish at a touch). He hung up his battledress in
the musty wardrobe, slipped into bed and for two minutes lay
with the light off staring upwards into darkness; then turned at
last on his side and allowed his trim and not much over forty
bachelor's body to slip directly into sleep.

'And how are we this morning, gentlemen?' the publican
inquired of Dalby and Winters at breakfast. He was holding
out an envelope. 'Telegram. The boy forgot to give it to you last
night.' Winters took it and nodded a minimal thanks. 'Guess
*someone* knows where you are anyway,' the publican added with
sympathy. Winters had it open now. *SUGGEST FLYING RALLY
AT GERADGERY TOMORROW TO COUNTER BENTON.
BARKER.*

Though Geradgery was too small to have figured more than
once on the maze of their itinerary so far, Winters remembered
that occasion very well. Effectively it had begun in Armidale
with his friend Barker's disquiet over his vicar and culminated
with that strangely disarming tone the vicar himself had used at
the rally. In print the words might have been sound enough but
something in their delivery suggested now the mockery which
later events had shown them to be. That 'widows and orphans'
reference ... Though there had been much more distressing
events in the following months, that rally at Geradgery had
marked, when he considered it, the onset of his troubles. Not
that the man had been sinister. Hardly. It was more a naiveté.
Everything, according to Benton (he remembered the name
even without the telegram), might suddenly be simpler than
you'd ever imagined.

And all this had been months before the man had actually
delivered the travesty of a sermon that Barker had talked of
with Winters a fortnight ago on his way north. The bishop

and his wife rather liked having the captain to stay on his way through and Winters, though doubtful at first, did not protest. Tonight, in fact, would be another such occasion—port and conversation, surmises on the Western Front. But now in Tenterfield, as the memory of Benton regained its shape, the thought of such a sermon was more jarring than a whole day of ungiven salutes, a total denial of all that the clergy stood for. Births, deaths and marriages, Christmas and Easter—that was the preserve Winters' father had kept them to. And they'd come willingly enough out to the homestead when required, not quite employees, but not quite anything else either.

'Bad news, captain?' asked Dalby, pouring a second cup of tea.

'Change of plan, sergeant.' Dalby waited. Nothing at Gallipoli had disposed him to question an officer, despite his quiet irritation at their occasionally English airs. The captain abruptly pushed back his chair and smiled. 'We'll do a matinee at Geradgery on the way through.' Then already he was on his way to the hotel office. Leaving his tea unfinished, Dalby got up and set off unevenly between the tables out into the yard to the car. Winters with a single bang on the office bell had brought the publican running.

## 30

Outside the town's most northerly cottage Dalby swung the Packard over and, under the impassive but watchful eye of a small boy safe on his veranda, fixed a flag to the mast on the radiator cap, then tied a pair of calico banners to the rear doors and another, larger one on the back over the spare wheel. *JOIN THE A.I.F. ENLIST NOW,* read the boy's mother, attracted by the unchanging metre of the idling engine. A few seconds later, and four hundred yards up the road, they heard the first blast on the horn.

Still honking, Dalby drew the car up abruptly outside the post office. With minimum movement he lifted a small portable dais from the back seat and set it squarely down on the footpath. When his sergeant had been standing neatly at ease for some moments Winters, with suitable military stiffness, got out and mounted his podium. He had an audience of a dozen or so, mainly women, won by the horn's insistence, its sheer flagrance in the still mid-afternoon. They stared at the big print and admired the polish of the captain's appearance—mature admittedly, but a man to embody their ideal soldier, a fraction undersize, maybe, but the slant of his cap and the cut of his moustache more than made up for that.

There was a further professional pause and then, as if the crowd might just as well be twenty thousand as twenty, Winters began. The need for notes had gone long since; the exhortation flowed—mechanical and dependable as the Packard behind him with its summary of his message. An inner circle of older women formed and held as an outer rim half-circled around it. Three or four children just out from school wondered at the Packard's bonnet and threatened at any moment to mount the running board and fiddle with the steering. Dalby, uncomfortably at ease beside the little dais, moved only his eyes, ignoring the children and holding a moment separately each eligible man as he broke away up the street.

'Any young man,' Winters was saying, his voice full of energy yet not far from exhaustion, 'who calls himself a man, will volunteer now before conscription makes him—and be proud to join the hundred thousand already in France. The peril of this country and the peril of the Empire have never been greater. Yes, we may be thankful for the Royal Navy's triumph at Jutland, but if Britain goes down, then so does Australia, let us be certain on that.'

Two young men, who, unlike the others, did not appear to have anything more pressing to do, worked their way through to the inner circle; silent at first—then, as Winters wound towards his climax, giving sharp grunts of approval. Though the captain rarely particularised his appeals or studied faces, he found himself this time focused tightly on the two of them. There was a rare confidence there, a recklessness even. It was a quality Winters saw now almost with relief. Both were of a height, six foot maybe, a pair of front row forwards. They looked familiar but not enough to actually greet. It was the face he knew, more than the individuals: freckled, pale but reddened, coarsened a little by the wind—landowners' sons, to go from the clothes.

'So if any of you lads have decided to join, just stay behind a moment here and give your names to Sergeant Dalby—a genuine veteran of the Dardanelles, if you didn't know. And there's always a week allowed before you go, of course, to get your affairs settled and so on.'

Winters by now had scaled his tone right down and was in effect talking directly to the two young men, virtually the only two of the audience left anyway. As the last of the crowd and even the children shifted away, a couple of shopkeepers came up incuriously to congratulate the captain on his address and wonder how things were going. The sergeant meanwhile was reaching out a sort of ledger from the back seat of the car. Then, uncapping a fountain pen from his battledress pocket, he said: 'What's your names then, lads?'

'McEwan,' announced the first, almost as if he should know already. 'Barry McEwan.'

'M-a-c or M-c?'

'M-c-capital E-w-a-n, from Gilandra, via Ebor.' He spelled that out too. 'You're on the lucky side, you blokes,' McEwan went on as Dalby got down the last of the details. 'You could have missed us altogether. We were all fixed to join up next weekend with a mate of ours from school down in Sydney. Turns out he's already gone though—just got word yesterday.' The tone irritated Dalby, an unnerving mixture of naivety and condescension.

'So when you blokes came rolling in we thought we might as well get started here and now.' At close range Dalby saw the other one was just a fraction less keen but there was no gainsaying the decision. Dalby looked at him with some approval. A measure of caution was better in the long run. There were quite a few like this McEwan still at Gallipoli who needn't have been, lieutenants mostly.

'Fine decision, lads,' said Captain Winters, striding over from his merchants to shake the two boys by the hand. 'Finest body of men in the Allied armies. You should do them proud.' Winters' grandiloquence seemed to embarrass the second youth—who turned to Dalby to give his name.

'Ian Pinson, Anneslie, via Ebor,' spelling it out as the other two waited.

'Well, that's about it then,' said McEwan chirpily. 'How about a drink on it, sir? We've still got that week to sort ourselves out after all.' Seeing Winters' astonishment, he pressed on: 'I'm sure old George at the Royal will stand us a drink or two on the strength of this. What do you say, captain?' The boy was an upstart certainly—by personality if not by class—but at least he'd volunteered, which was more than could be said for all but one of the fit young men of Tenterfield. He remembered the hotel room there, the flounced and irritating curtains, the report he'd posted that morning to Head Office before leaving, its brief appendix of recruits. He looked again at the young face. 'What do you say, captain?' It should have been insolence but suddenly Winters couldn't see why not. They weren't due in Armidale till seven and that was only thirty miles on after all. Both Pinson and Dalby looked less certain. Dalby had never quite been allowed to forget it was only his presence at Gallipoli that got him a drink with the captain, a privilege which, in any case, he did not rank highly. Pinson, for his part, was muttering something about not having loaded up the stuff from Elder's yet.

As Dalby stacked away the dais and rolled up the signs, the two recruits and Winters stood by and established that in fact the captain's family had a property at Muswellbrook and that McEwan and he had some distant cousin in common. McEwan also tested Winters a little about the Packard. 'No way it'd beat an Olds, I reckon. We've had ours up to seventy on a good stretch up near Glen Innes there.' Then with Dalby ready at last and lagging slightly they set off up the street for the Royal. Winters, surveying the saloon bar on entry, noted with satisfaction its panelled interior, the photograph of King George, the etchings of blood horses at full stretch and the COME OVER HERE, BOYS, YOU'RE WANTED poster with its bandaged arm beckoning. An Australian flag and the Union Jack stretched side by side high on the far wall.

'What'll it be, gentlemen?'

'Four beers, George—and it's on you this time. Ian and I have just joined up, just like we said, remember? We're off next week, so how about it?' George, a sallow forty-five with thinning hair, looked less than impressed. McEwan plunged on. 'This gentleman here is Captain Winters ... and this is Sergeant Dalby, late of Gallipoli, in fact.'

'Pleased to meet you,' said George, looking a little

embarrassed, as much for the soldiers as himself. He turned to McEwan. 'What's your father say?' he asked in a tone which might as well have been questioning whether he was old enough to drink.

'Been on the cards for quite a while. No problem there. Young Billy can always come up out of school if he has to. Now what about those drinks?'

Winters rapped impatiently with his swagger stick against his shoe. 'I'll have a Scotch, if you don't mind—and make it a shandy for the sergeant here.' McEwan stared at the close-shaven back of George's neck as he filled the order. Dalby said nothing. A shandy, apparently, was all right with him.

'How's it been going then, sir?' said Pinson at last, as if to furnish the deference McEwan lacked. 'Bit of a rush before next Saturday, I guess. A lot of our over twenty-fives are down at the Armidale camp with the Home Service call-up—just waiting the O.K., I reckon.'

'Didn't quite get down to us eighteen year olds,' said McEwan, one foot on the footrail and still watching George. 'Not that we'd've gone chasing exemptions like some people we know.' He looked around at Winters. 'Makes you wonder, doesn't it?'

'No way a fellow can stay at home with things in France the way they are,' said Pinson. Winters still said nothing. He had gone far enough already. It was as if only the arrival of a drink would give him speech.

'You can say that again,' said McEwan. George at last had set down the drinks—on the house, as requested. McEwan turned, leaned back on the bar and lifted his glass. 'Here's to us then— and not a moment too soon either.' He turned back to George with a deliberate smile which was not reciprocated. 'And thank you, George, for being such a gentleman,' he said with an edge of irony. 'A real mate, eh, Ian?'

Pinson stared silently down at the footrail. Winters, staring at the floor, sensed something he couldn't name pass between them, this youth and the barman. 'We'll see what the army makes of him, eh, captain?' He looked up, having caught only the rank.

'What's that?'

'I said it'll be good to see the army sort him out a bit. Been a bit of a tearaway, bit of a problem, this young fellow, one way or another.' McEwan gave a shallow laugh.

'Now look here, George, I thought we had an understanding, you and me.' The bartender gave McEwan something less than a smile.

'Well, this is it, then,' said Pinson awkwardly into the silence. Suddenly, without reason, all three looked at Dalby, at the paleness of his shandy.

'Let's sit down,' said the sergeant, heading off towards a table under the flags. It seemed somehow to be an order. All three obeyed.

## 31

The captain glanced at his watch as McEwan came across from the bar waving another pair of schooners. He could feel Dalby, still nursing his shandy, wince beside him. At five o'clock now it was clear, or almost clear, that condescension had gone far enough. He looked up and saw the barman thought so too.

'Actually,' said McEwan slopping the drinks down and taking up where he'd left off, 'all these bloody parsons are a bit pathetic if you ask me. That chaplain at school, for instance. You remember, Ian. Old "Creeping Jesus". He was hopeless.'

'Now listen to me, lad,' said Winters abruptly, irritated rather than soothed by his three inexplicable whiskies. 'You should show the church a little respect. The bishop here, as it happens, is a personal friend of mine. One of the best schoolboy footballers in England, he was—and a great supporter of recruitment, as you ought to know.'

'Yeah,' said McEwan, undeterred. 'Well, that's as maybe but you ought to see the one we got around here though. He'd lick the Kaiser's arse if given the instruction. You should have heard him talking with that Wobbly bunch down at the post office last week. Vote NO he reckoned and bring the boys home. Never mind about Belgium or anything like that. Just wrap it up and head off. That's what he said, wasn't it, Ian? You were there, for Christ's sake.' Winters pushed back his chair and looked again at his watch. He could feel Dalby's respect for him withering by the minute.

'Yeah,' said Pinson abstractedly, almost as if the two men in uniform had never been there. 'He did seem pretty weak on it, if you ask me. Bit gutless really.'

'What do you mean gutless? It wasn't much short of—what

do you call it? Treason, yeah. Standing there as large as life
telling every bastard passing by that it wasn't the Lord's will
they should join up and Jesus had told him personally that a
NO vote was required on this occasion.' McEwan took a long
suck at his beer. 'Makes you sick to think about it.'

Winters was on his feet at last. The common cousin, the
properties down the line, the afternoon's recruitment, had been
too much presumed upon. Drunk or sober, this kind of talk
would scarcely pass with an N.C.O., let alone an officer.

'Gee, sir, you're not going, are you? You've only had a couple.
It's only a bit after five. A man doesn't join up every day, you
know.' McEwan started to stand up, not quite knocking over
his beer. 'You don't mind—I was only talking about the local
bloke.'

'Yes,' said Winters as McEwan sat back heavily in his chair, 'I
can see that. And I hold no brief for the man myself but if I were
you, McEwan, I'd finish this all up now and get yourself down
to camp as soon as you can. That's where you'll be most use to
us, after all.'

This, apparently, was the sergeant's view, too, for he already
had withdrawn towards the door. The boy had obviously missed
out on a good hiding somewhere—one week in Holsworthy
would set him right soon enough. Winters, however, could
not make the break so readily. Now as if nothing at all had
intervened since the rally two hours back, the captain thrust
his hand out to the two youths and wished them luck. He took
the stickiness of the spilt beer with him on his palm to the car.
Sergeant Dalby held back the door for the captain and followed
him out without looking back. There was a sudden patch of
light, then nothing.

'Just don't worry about it,' McEwan was saying, two hours and
five schooners later. 'Sit down. The old man's not really gonna
mind. It's only a roll of barbed wire, for Christ's sake. We'll be
seeing plenty of that before we're through.' Pinson had got to his

feet as if this might in itself waken some blurred responsibility in McEwan too.

'Sit down,' McEwan ordered, grabbing firmly the tail of Pinson's sportscoat. Pinson slid back into his chair, banging the table sideways. The two empty glasses rattled but did not fall. 'That's better, mate. Now listen. I got an idea. Mighta been nice to have the captain in on it but ...' McEwan lifted his glass and seemed surprised to see it empty. 'Just a little bit of unfinished business, you might say.' Pinson ran a finger through a pool on the table. 'You know what I mean, that bloody streak of a clergyman, or excuse for one. No wonder old Barker stood him down.' Pinson began to see now; he looked round at McEwan with deliberate slowness. 'He's still up there though—sort of shepherd without his prize merinos, as it were. Somebody ought to defrock him, that's the term, isn't it, debag the bastard. What do you reckon, Ian? Teach the Kaiser's bum boy a lesson before we go.'

'I don't know, Barry.' Pinson stared hard at the opposite wall, remembering only a year ago a couple of bare-arsed first formers running round in tears, their trousers tossed on the covered way roof. There were others too who'd had their heads stuffed down toilets in the middle of prep. A longstanding threat of expulsion had never quite arrived.

'What do you mean you don't bloody know?'

'Well ...'

'Well, nothing. He's a Boche, isn't he? Or as good as anyway.'

'You know, I still think we ought to ...' began Pinson. McEwan seemed neither to hear nor understand.

'We'll just take a leak first,' he said and that seemed to settle it. Pinson followed him out to the gents where they stood, swaying a little, spraying the porcelain up and down as if painting a wall. Without quite realising it, Pinson was waiting for a touch of McEwan braggadocio, but checking sideways saw only sober concentration. Then, suddenly, McEwan had finished and called from the door before plunging out: 'See you at the car, mate. Just had an idea. Old George might be able to help us on this one. He owes me a favour.'

Pinson shook himself dry, stared awhile in the mirror, rinsed his hands and made his way back through to the bar. As he walked past, half looking to nod his thanks to George, he noticed the counter unattended. Then, stepping out into the evening light, he strolled across the road towards the car—and the shut doors of Elder Smiths, the barbed wire in the window.

'Hey, Ian, give us a hand, you bastard!' He looked back to see McEwan, in this light a shape only, bent sharply to the left by a dead weight at the end of his arm. He also appeared to be clutching a large bag across his chest.

'What've you got there, you silly bastard?' called Pinson, heading back.

'Just a little present from George. Nice bloke, that George. Here, hang onto this.'

Pinson took the four gallon tin which he could just see was unlabelled. It was heavier than he expected. 'Hey, kero wasn't on the ...'

'It's honey, you dumb bugger,' said McEwan, his voice dulled by the large chaff bag he was still hugging in front of him.

'Yeah, but ...'

'Just to sweeten things up a little.' With no further question Pinson swung the tin in over the back door and got out the crank handle. McEwan tossed the bag in the back too and slipped in smoothly behind the wheel. The engine caught first try.

'Let's bloody go then,' called McEwan as Pinson swung round into the passenger seat and the Oldsmobile surged out into the street and headed south.

Though the sun had gone the light was still there, a violet haze. Pinson sat back and watched the blur of shopfronts and verandas as McEwan ripped through the gears. It was only four blocks to the church. Halfway there Pinson began: 'You know, Barry ...'

'What's the problem? He's a Hun, isn't he? Just as good as.'

Then the big car in a single fluid movement swerved right
then left and bounced up the vicarage drive. Parallel beams
swept the squares of the front window. The engine raced and
cut. McEwan leaned over the back of his seat and picked up a
long, bent shape from the floor. There was a metallic snap. 'Just
might come in handy,' he said, embracing the chaff bag with his
other hand. 'You bring the sweetener,' he called back over his
shoulder, striding already for the door.

## 32

Benton, reading in the drawing room before dinner the *Herald*'s account of Saturday's rally (*a crowd of approximately eight hundred*) had heard the sounds without really sensing their meaning: the two turns in off the road, the flamboyant halt in the drive. Then after the engine soared and cut, some muffled instructions and, almost immediately, the banging on his door. Though he shrank a little at such brutal succession, a habit much deeper raised him from his chair towards the door.

Though there were only two of them, the doorway filled with their reddened faces. There was a moment in which none of the three spoke and Benton's mind raced backwards to recall them. Midday sun ... the post office steps ... one on a horse, leaning down from the saddle; the smell he knew too from that morning in the Royal, a concentrate of it.

'Just like a little word with you, reverend,' said McEwan in a tone which ignored the double-barrelled twelve gauge hanging loosely from his right hand and glinting in the light from the hall. It pointed, almost casually, at Benton's shoes. 'Seeing as we've just joined up and all.'

'But I really don't see ...' said Benton, reaching back for the edge of the door.

'Just a little word, Mr Benton.' The gun swung up towards Benton's belly as both youths took a step forward. 'Don't worry about the sweetener just yet, Ian,' said McEwan, following Benton closely as he backed sideways across the hall into the drawing room.

'Well, Barry ...' said Benton, the name, the baptism, coming back to him now: that reluctant adolescent in the family photo outside the chapel later. Mrs McEwan had sent him one 'as a record'.

'Well, Mr Benton,' said McEwan, neatly parodying the minister's tone, 'it seems you don't know much about the Hun, do you? Judging from what you had to say down at the post office last week.' The shotgun wavered vaguely across Benton's lower abdomen. Pinson stood by the door to the hall awaiting orders. Benton was hard against the sofa now, the fumes of alcohol less shocking but lending the whole room volatility. Their drunkenness, Benton could see (though he knew little of these things), was enough to lessen inhibition but not enough to give an enemy advantage. He thought again, as he'd done from the first moment, of Amy and Billyjim down in the kitchen and flirted with the idea of knocking the gun aside and taking both youths on by hand.

'You didn't read about the bayoneted babies, the massacred priests, I suppose?' McEwan's voice slipped into the grating self-righteous register of the boarding school bully. Pinson looked warily down the hall.

'Hey, Barry, it's the bloody wife and kid!' This, Pinson's voice suggested, was not part of the routine at school—nor for that matter was the shotgun.

'Just let 'em come, mate. All the better.'

Pinson backed into the room, almost pushed aside by Amy holding Billyjim in her arms.

'David, what on ...?' Amy, Benton saw, must have intuited something like this on her way up the hall but the shotgun, as it swung towards her, had not been part of it.

'Just stand over there in the corner, Mrs,' McEwan advised, 'and you won't get hurt. We're just about to ask your husband here a few leading questions, as they say.' Benton had been watching her wide, open face from that moment in the doorway when she registered how things were. She also sniffed the alcohol and seemed to toy with some desperate move before, with a look at David, abandoning it for better sense. Benton saw too the pale incomprehension in his son's face before he turned away towards his mother's throat. Benton looked at her helplessly as Billyjim began to sob.

He turned to McEwan, angry now but cautious. 'I'm sure we can discuss this in a civilised manner, Barry. Why don't you just put that thing down and we'll say no more about it, eh?'

'Civilised manner, eh?' sneered McEwan. 'That's a good one. Sounds like the Hun—very smart.' He lifted the barrel a little. 'There's nothing very civilised about ratting on your country and calling it religion. Sounds pretty bloody funny to me.' With a spare part of his mind Benton was wondering where he got his phraseology—the Royal saloon? The word 'religion' reminded him obscurely of how much had slipped away. 'Here,' said McEwan to his friend, 'keep this trained on the kid.' They fumbled the changeover just enough for Benton to feel the opportunity flash and vanish when he might have rushed them, but Pinson had the gun steady now and pointed at the boy.

As McEwan skipped out the door Benton, from where he was against the sofa, could see him framed by darkness. And over the rhythms of his son's sobbing he heard Amy saying to Pinson: 'Why don't you stop it right now? You know he's only bullying you as much as he is us. You've got the gun. You don't want to go to gaol just for ...'

'Just shut up, Mrs,' said Pinson almost plaintively. 'We're pretty bloody shickered if you want to know ... and it's loaded, I can tell you that much.' Benton, even through his own anxiety and anger, could feel how much the big, bemused boy was wishing it finished. Why had McEwan disappeared? Some further schoolboy elaborations? Or would the engine leap to life and disappear?

Then McEwan, in a half-stooping run, came back through the door, dragging what seemed like a kerosene tin and a full chaff bag. In the middle of the room he bent over the tin and twisted off the lid.

'Thought we might have the captain in on this,' he said,

looking up at Benton. 'Only he shot through at the last minute. Not a good example to the troops, eh?' Benton stared at the kerosene tin, remembering the liquid's usefulness in starting a copper.

'You're not ...' said Benton, waiting for the smell to hit him.

'Don't worry, no fire and brimstone—just a little sweetener and a little chaff instead of white feathers. McEwan's Sure-Fire Miracle Cure for Local Huns, what do you reckon, Ian?' Pinson obliged with a sheepish laugh. 'Now if you'll just take off your pants, or is it a frock in this case?' McEwan, dragging the tin closer, glanced up at Pinson for the expected laugh but the allusion proved obscure. Still Benton made no move; his eyes travelled the invisible line between Pinson's shotgun and Billyjim's backbone. The boy was sobbing uncontrollably now, as if standing in a cot in a dark room across the hall and getting no reply.

'You want us to shut that kid up, once and for all?'

Benton finally looked down directly into McEwan's eyes, trying to gauge his drunkenness, his determination. 'You better get a bit closer there, Ian,' McEwan went on, beginning to lift the tin and not looking at Pinson. 'He's not so good on ducks and rabbits, this bloke, but he's not likely to miss at two yards.' Pinson stepped in closer as ordered. Amy was right back against the bookshelves now.

'Now get your clothes off quick.' Till now only the most practical thoughts had been occurring to Benton: the lamp on the mantelpiece—could he knock it out? Could he wrestle with McEwan and risk the other's indecision? Now, without his reaching for it, the image of Christ's nakedness and scourging presented itself—that *template of integrity*, as he'd said somewhere. Strange how Christ and his twelve were men without children. He looked again at the shotgun and started to undo his belt. As the cooler air hit first his legs and then his torso he saw, as he stood there, tall and white, his clothes a swift obliging heap on the floor beside him, how else it might have been. Meeting Amy's eyes he saw her naked, those ample breasts and generous thighs, her pubic V a focal point, and three men (himself included) staring. The nakedness between them had been a separate world, existing only in bed and not even shared with Billyjim. He looked down and away from her, hearing the small echo of that word 'violation' from communiqués and seeing the incongruous circle of his celluloid collar surmounting his thrown-down clothes.

'Down on the sofa.' Again Benton could not quite move, though he had the smell straight now. A slanting sunlight kind of smell, totally out of place. McEwan seemed increasingly to hurry and be rather put out, as if he'd intended something more elaborate, some pseudo-legal dialectic which he would win and thus make what he had in mind a proper sentence and not the mere violence it was becoming.

'Down on the sofa, I said.' Pinson numbly swung the gun towards Benton to get him moving. Amy started a rush for the door but Pinson brought her up short with both barrels pressed into Billyjim's back. The boy, who'd suddenly stopped crying as Amy moved, howled again.

'No,' said Pinson, an edge of panic in his voice. Amy backed away slightly as Benton, seeing no alternative, at last placed himself face downwards on the sofa.

'That's better,' said McEwan, seeming to recover his nerve and lifting the tin again. 'Wouldn't want anything to go wrong, would we? He's had a few too many, that feller. Anything could happen.'

Benton, his face pressed sideways against the sofa's fabric, saw Amy turn from what was about to happen, sheltering Billyjim from the line of fire. Then Benton shivered as the honey with its storeroom coolness started to run in a thick stream from shoulder to ankle, running down over his back onto the sofa and down between his buttocks. He could feel the pulse of its exit from the tin and the way it worked down round his scrotum.

'Other side, you bloody Hun,' said McEwan, his voice thick with an almost sexual tension. 'Other bloody cheek, if you like.' Benton rolled over as if to a doctor's examination. He could see Amy's shoulders and, two yards off, the divisions at work in the other one's face, the shotgun itself so much more decided than its wielder. He clamped his teeth and stared up into the stretched, pale face of McEwan as the tin again moved above him. A steady two inch stream throbbed from its mouth, advancing upwards from his feet, still in their black socks. McEwan's eyes followed its course exactly, abstracted and inward, akin, Benton realised suddenly, in their self-absorption, to the inexorable moment of seminal release. As the honey moved up from his chest onto his face, his mouth, his nostrils and his eyes, a pure, limitless anger at last suffused him. Half-blinded with honey he leapt up from the sofa and swung out wildly, grunting an obscenity he'd not heard since school and never used himself. He heard rather than saw the kerosene tin thump to the floor.

'C'mon, Ian, let's go—that ought to teach the bastard. Better leave the chaff. Fucking pacifist's got himself all worked up.' One set of feet moved away from him. 'Come on—don't just stand there.' Benton, though his eyes were still sealed with honey, could see the other one's dazed face whisked sideways through the door and felt his anger, pure as it was, swing through to relief as he realised there'd been no explosion, no Martini-Henry ringing in his ears. He started for where Amy must still be in the corner near the bookcase and tripped immediately over the chaff bag. The next moment Amy was helping him up with her free hand and, with Billyjim still sobbing, drew him towards her, pushing her face hard against his and the honey which still covered it, bringing the child in too. They stood there together almost two minutes, as twice outside the crank handle failed to start a spark and Billyjim's sobbing lessened. Benton stood right up now, attempting to blink the honey from his eyes, feeling down the backs of his legs its slow descent to the floor. Only slowly did he become aware of the paradox of his nakedness against the enveloping folds of Amy's dress, now also streaked with honey. Outside, through the open door, with astonishing closeness, the big motor finally caught; the car roared backwards down the drive out onto the street; then raced away northwards.

*Suffer ye thus far*, he recalled. *It is enough.* He could hear the resonance of it now and see himself declaring it once more from the pulpit, naked and running with honey, Mrs Giddins in the front row looking up, Cyril Somerton behind him in the choir. He thought of the receding car and how far and where it might finally take them, of his mother out there at Wallagundah watching saucepans on a stove and of Jack near Pozières somewhere dissolving under his makeshift cross, of the rising laughter down at the Royal ('... turned the other cheek, they reckon') and the impassive face of Rawson at his desk at the police station and how the vote might go on Saturday, the thousands of young men already in camp awaiting consignment. *Suffer ye thus far. It is enough.* He stooped again and drew his family to him, eyes clearing with tears.

# PART FOUR

PART FOUR

## 33

'Belvedere',
Raglan Street,
Geradgery N.S.W.
30.9.17

Dear Mrs Bartrim,

May I say on my own behalf and that of the Guild how sad I
was to see your dear Johnny's name in the Herald yesterday. He
was a fine lad and I well remember his exemplary politeness at the
counter and, of course, his prowess on the tennis courts. The club at
St Jude's has never had anyone to equal him, before or since. It seems
this Battle of the Menin Road has played a vital role and I'm sure it
is a great consolation to you to know that his sacrifice has not been
in vain.

I do apologise for not having written earlier but as a former Guild
member during this great conflict you'll know how things have
been. It's almost a year now, isn't it? I hope you and Mr Bartrim are
prospering there at Strathfield as you did here. The store these days,
I'm afraid, is not what it was in your time; very understocked and
the service leaves much to be desired. It's all you can do now to buy
decent soap.

The Guild, needless to say, was very sorry to see you leave,
especially at such a difficult time, what with my own resignation
and all, but not long after the referendum (and the timely departure
of that man Benton) we put things back together again rather
nicely. The dean (what an impressive man he is!) stood in for some
weeks until our new man got back from overseas, a Reverend Philip
Watkins, a strapping young fellow who'd just completed a tour of
duty as chaplain with the Second Division. Compared to Benton,
he's outstanding indeed even if a little taciturn perhaps (no wife,

as yet), but at least there's no doubt where he stands on the King and Country issue as there was with his predecessor. A disgraceful episode altogether, that. I'm not sure if you ever heard the full story, leaving as you did, I remember, that weekend before the big vote (and how its result still makes me boil: 12,000 NO to 7,000 YES in our own electorate! You can't tell me our Mr Benton didn't have something to do with that!).

Actually I'm not even sure I know the real story. There were a couple going around; you never quite find out the truth in these things. One was that he and Bishop Barker had actually come to fisticuffs in the bishop's study as he was handing in his resignation (Miss Pym is said to have seen something like this). The other is a kind of 'tar-and-feathering' story. I don't know if you remember young Barry McEwan and Ian Pinson (not great churchgoing families but well known in the district even so). Apparently the same night they enlisted (inspired to do so by that grand recruiter Capt. Winters, whom I'm sure you'll remember) they had a little too much to drink at the Royal and I understand (though it's not openly said) that they drove up to the vicarage and, rather than 'tar-and-feather' him (as they might have done in the old days) they 'honey-and-chaffed' him, as it were. They say George Emery at the Royal and even Capt. Winters had something to do with it; though I very much doubt the latter. Of course, I don't hold with that sort of thing myself but I must say it did rather amuse me. That clerical scarecrow with his lofty ideas, so far above the clouds and the rest of us. Never win the war with his attitudes, turning the Gospel about like that.

I did feel rather sorry for his wife though, a nice young thing, as you remember, who I took quite a personal interest in actually— though she never seemed quite as friendly as she might have been. Quite distressing it must have been for her but I doubt if he's changed his spots at all—though it must have taught him something of a lesson, I dare say. He didn't lodge any charges, we noticed. He'd not get much help from our good Sergeant Rawson there, I expect; though I suppose that must have had something to do with why our two young lads left so soon after signing up instead of taking their week or so as most of the boys have.

Anyway, whatever happened, he resigned his ministry the next week (as well he might what with the bishop having already withdrawn his licence, as you'd recall) and left for Sydney. I heard someone say he's teaching down there somewhere (a fine example to young people, I must say!) and working with the I.W.W., the Sinn Feiners and others of that ilk. Good to see our Billy making noises again about another referendum though, isn't it? We'll give them a run for their money this time! And in the meantime the Guild and I must keep up our morale—and our sterling contribution to the Comforts Fund; 6,000 pairs in our Sock Drive this year and a special certificate to hang in the parish hall.

Must be off now to cut some poppies for the church. Everything's a little early this year and the gardens all over will soon be looking splendid. Mr Watkins is very appreciative of my efforts, I must say (not many flowers in no-man's-land, I suppose). More appreciative certainly than that Benton fellow ever was (he hardly knew what day it was, let alone which flower!).

And do let me say again how sorry we all were here to learn of Johnny's death. Please accept our sincerest condolences.

Yours sincerely,
Joyce Giddins

P.S. I knew in my bones there was a reason not to send this yesterday. Now in this morning's Express I see that both the McEwan boy and the Pinson boy have been killed. Makes you wonder, doesn't it: the flower of our youth cut down so bravely while eligibles still slack at home (or fiddle God's Word to suit their stripes!). Do write.

This print edition published in collaboration with Brio Books,
an imprint of Booktopia Group Ltd

Level 6, 1A Homebush Bay Drive · Rhodes NSW 2138 · Australia

Print ISBN: 9781761281167

briobooks.com.au

The paper in this book is FSC® certified.
FSC® promotes environmentally responsible,
socially beneficial and economically viable
management of the world's forests.